The Campaign Trail

Francis Nji Bangsi

Langaa Research & Publishing CIG
Mankon, Bamenda

Publisher
Langaa RPCIG
Langaa Research & Publishing Common Initiative Group
P.O. Box 902 Mankon
Bamenda
North West Region
Cameroon
Langaagrp@gmail.com
www.langaa-rpcig.net

Distributed in and outside N. America by African Books Collective
orders@africanbookscollective.com
www.africanbookcollective.com

ISBN: 9956-717-35-5

DISCLAIMER
All views expressed in this publication are those of the author and do
not necessarily reflect the views of Langaa RPCIG.

Dedication

To Siga Asanga,
My teacher and mentor.
RIP

Chapter One

Kutuma was not a vast country. Its capital, Fusejo, was a semi-urban settlement with an agrarian outlook, which had gained prominence when the first colonial explorers came to settle there and to explore its mineral depots. In terms of topography, it seems as if nature upon creation had gathered all the hills, mountains, rivers and deep valleys in this part of the world. But for its capital town, the settlements, some of which came to be known as Administrative divisions, had very difficult access. Such units were created after independence in areas where the population density was high enough. The many hills, valleys and big rivers made communication very difficult. The colonial masters had some roads dug manually to link up the mainland to the mineral depots.

The fertility of the land remained a blessing to the people of Kutuma. When a seed dropped even close to a rock it grew to its full length and resulted in produce of high quality. This gave the vast expanse of land greenery that was quite pleasing to behold. Freshness was observable everywhere.

This fertility was not limited to crops; it was reflected even in the procreation of Kutuma citizens. Most of the young women were mothers of twins, otherwise known as "magnis" in local parlance. One woman gave birth to as many as a dozen children. In this society, children were considered as wealth. Children provided labour for farm work. The girl child was a double blessing, for when she was given out in marriage the father enjoyed bride price and the mother received lots of material gifts. The more children one had the higher one's social prestige. There was enough fertile farmland to produce food for all. Men of substance married many wives and with social stability the population expanded exponentially.

The mines and fertility had attracted the white man long ago and he came along with his church, his government, his school and his way of life. These influences were like a chemical reaction in strong palm wine. Our story is set in the Republic that gradually emerged over time from this chemical reaction between cultures.

Travelling from the National Headquarters, Fusejo, to any of the administrative units, especially in the rainy season was nightmarish. Indeed only a few of these units were linked up by motorable tracks. Most of the tracks had been created merely by the repeated cruising of motor tyres on the bushes of Kutuma. The first and last attempt at road construction was made through the laborious input of the natives, using their hands and crude implements under the command of the white overseers. A caterpillar had never been used to open up a road. The only earth road done with a touch of engineering was one that led to the mines. Since these roads never received any maintenance, a distance of 5 kilometres sometimes took two whole days of untold suffering to its travellers. The ordeal was unbearable, especially in the heart of the rainy season when the roads became slippery. The passengers would occasionally climb down and push for hours to free the vehicle when it got stuck in mud. This was the case for villages fortunate enough to have such an access. The only all-season vehicles that could dare it on such roads were the "*line lobbers*" as the Land Rover mark was pronounced by the villagers.

Other localities could only be reached by hard trekking. There were areas which had obstacles such as large rivers and stretches of boulders. In these areas the people eased communication by building hanging rope and bamboo bridges, a real feat of traditional engineering. It was believed that these bridges were done by specialists initiated into a riverine meant for that purpose. The complicated patterns of weaving seen in these ropes clearly lent authenticity to this belief. Thanks to such initiatives, it was possible to bring in industrial provision to the peoples of the hinterland though everything was transported by head-load. When such basic commodities finally got there, most of the local retailers would sell them at high cost owing to the transportation difficulties.

The colonial power was greatly attracted to the mineral deposits of Kutuma. The people, who lived in total ignorance of such potentials, saw the white man as a mad man, tilling into rocks for the unknown. At first the exploiters brought gifts to the traditional rulers, and then they made away with whatever quantities of resources they could afford to carry. Little did the people know that these precious elements would come to have an impact on the citizens. Life went on in native Kutuma, with no regard to these national resources. In as much as the people ate to satisfaction and drank his traditional liquor, brewed from corn or tapped from the bamboo sieves, he celebrated the joy of living and lived in harmony with his environment.

As the colonial influence grew stronger, a new elitist group with education and increased political awareness sprang up. They saw the need to pressure for independence. This was a generation of young people, most of whom were primary school teachers, who had read about political changes in neighbouring nations and were up-to-date with the news from the radio. Some smart ones felt that Kutuma could not stay indifferent in a world of political change where many neighbouring nations were asserting self-governance. For this idea to make sense to a people who did not care whether the white man remained there till eternity or not, a lot of explanation was needed on the advantages that could come from self-governance. A man who ate well, slept well, drank well and enjoyed his wife had no reason to bother about the future. These elites, with their new visions, brought change to bear on the routine of traditional Kutuma. They started writing petitions to the United Nations and inviting their traditional leaders to sign, asking for autonomy of governance. Many neighbouring countries also struggled for this status. A positive reply to their request for independence was not easily obtained.

Chapter Two

No condition is permanent. At last the decision was reached at the United Nations for Kutuma to become an independent state. Many forces had contributed to this. Amongst them were the traditional rulers and the elite championed by Mr Utum Tar, the mission grade II headmaster. This good news was received with jubilation and became the main topic of discussion in most gatherings. Before the final talks that led to this independence, an invitation was sent to Kutuma for some selected persons to go to the UN. The night before their departure to New York, Utum Tar assembled the members of his delegation for final preparations and narrated to them a vision, which had visited his mind's eye. In the vision he had gone behind his house and, instead of the usual small coffee and plantain farm, he had seen a vast estate of infinite fertility and beauty. An invisible voice had told him that all of this land was going to be his provided he respected one condition. He was to enjoy abundance of procreation from plant to animal but he would not be allowed to eat a sumptuous meal throughout his lifetime. On the contrary, if he was presented with a rich meal, he should order his cooks to give it to the poor. His meals were to vary between parched corn, the local cassava puddle known as 'moyondo', parched ground-nuts or any other low nutrient diet. One day he was tempted to disobey this rule. Hunger had tempted him to go against this fast. His young newly-wedded wife, who did not understand why a man should torture himself with such a fasting as a means of further riches, tempted him with a sumptuous meal on a day when he returned home quite tired and hungry. No sooner had he violated this rule in his dream world, than a strange being, a horrible looking ogre descended from the sky and devoured everything on that fertile land. Barrenness immediately set in everywhere. His wife had blocked his way to becoming a very rich man. Every household suffered from severe starvation. Little children were all transformed into flat headed ogres, each one prepared to devour the other from lack of food.

Only a great diviner could make any sense of this strange dream. Only the first part of it mattered: one day there could be great prosperity. And this moment of independence was to usher in hope to the people of Kutuma who had never bothered about the white man's folly of tilling deep into their soil for the unknown. With some level of education, a few elite like Utum Tar had come to understand the value of the minerals which the white man was tapping from Kutuma land. Independence would, therefore, mean that a son of Kutuma would take the destiny of their land into his hands and utilise its natural potentials for the development of their country. Independence could stand for the start of the realisation of his dream.

This departure meeting was held at the *Fon*'s conference hall. The Fusejo Palace that hosted such important meetings had a rich history that had brought it to prominence. Kutuma, prior to any colonial arrangements, had its traditional government under its *Fons*. There were many of these *Fondoms* spreading into the hilly hinterlands. But the *Fon* of Fusejo, the capital, wielded particular influence because he was the first to receive the white man and because his dynasty descended from the legendary roots of the deity that founded this land. While the peoples differed slightly because of early migratory sources, they were united by one language, the Kutuma language, which was brought in by the now ruling dynasty. The colonial powers, much to the chagrin of other little chiefdoms, had come and given more powers to the host chief, pronouncing him as the paramount *Fon* since the mines were in his territory. History tells it that when the first white man came to this land, all the other *Fons* fled into hiding because they hadn't the courage to stand the awful sight of a burning man. This to them was not just a human being in the form of fire, but one with double eyes. In the local language this species of a creature was literally known as "the red man". The courageous person who accepted to go and be roasted by the red man was the *Fon* of Fusejo, who went and shook hands with the phenomenal being. This is how he made friends with the white man and came to be the mediator between him and the rest of the *Fons*. When the white man set up his government, he appointed him as paramount *Fon* and that is how he rose to prominence.

To prepare the delegation for a safe journey, the king enacted a special fare-well ritual. With a calabash of raffia wine in front of him and the horn in his right hand filled with wine, he started the incantation. After every pronouncement he poured some drops of wine on the floor:

"You are setting out for a hunt, may the gods of our land accompany you to the unknown and bring back everyone unscathed."

"May it be so," the people answered.

"If you meet a lion, may you be able to catch it with your bare hands and bring it home alive."

"May it be so."

"If you hit your foot against a stone, may that stone shatter into fragments while your foot stays unhurt."

"May it be so."

"We even hear that you will fly in a metallic bird. May none of its feathers pluck off, and may the headless *bgotoma* of

7

our dreaded deity smash any opponent that stands in your way spiritually to harm you on this trip!"

"May it be so."

Then he poured the final drop of libation on the ground and refilled his cup for the communion to take place. After a sip he called each member of the delegation to come forward and take his turn of the blessing. The first was Utum Tar, the steadfast activist for the independence struggle.

After all the departure formalities, the members set out on the journey in the metallic bird and were away for three weeks. In their period of absence, the local folk in their beer houses imagined things about the white man's land. Some said that the houses there were almost touching the sky. They wondered whether these architectural feats were the white man's search for God in the sky. Others described the eating habits there. They said that the white man ate raw grass and drank raw eggs. This sounded humorous for grass to the man of Kutuma was meant for cattle.

Chapter Three

The delegation from the United Nations was given a triumphant welcome back home. That morning crowds gathered at the Fusejo palace to get the news and see the heroes on their return trip. There was feasting along with traditional dances. At the chief's ceremonial ground, there were basins of *fufu*, vegetable and meat. When all the dignitaries had assembled, His Royal Highness the *Mbe* was ushered in by the trumpeting of the royal tusks. Then he sat majestically to receive his honours in a unanimous hand-clapping salutation from his country-men. When all was set, the master of ceremony, the celebrated teacher Utum Tar, got up with an immaculate white paper in hand. There was dead silence as he started to speak.

"We went, we saw, we touched, we won and we are back.. There was deafening applause. "Kutuma now is to be called the Republic of Kutuma! We are at last independent. As from this moment we have to rule ourselves. The white man who is here will remain as our guest and not as our master. This is a new dawn for our country." Many people clapped because they saw others clapping and not because they understood what self-government meant.

The next item on the agenda was the choice of a Head of State. When he read this out, the chief coughed in readiness to talk and, as he got up amidst honours of clapping, he proclaimed: "We do not have to delay on this point, my position is obvious. Teacher Tar is the right man. Do you doubt it?" The crowd responded once again in unison, "Teacher Utum Tar is our president." This is how the delegation's spokesman was indisputably consecrated as head of the new nation. This decision was saluted by more hand-clapping. Even *Fons* mistakenly clapped for him. This was indeed a reversal of roles because the common people usually clapped in reverence to the *Fon* and not the opposite. There would be many role reversals in the new nation. This coronation was given a traditional colouring. Strong witch doctors prepared a chain made of the strongest medicinal herbs to place round the neck of the newly crowned ruler. This gave him the desired protection. After the coronation of the President, it was time to settle down and give shape to the Republic. There was the great challenge of organising the institutions for the running of state affairs.

The first thing Utum Tar did was to appoint a foundation government made up of five key Ministries: Finance, Development, Defence, Education and Justice. This was a challenging task for him because his close collaborators in the colonial struggle were all looking to him for compensation. The *Fon* was given the post of First Technical Adviser to the President with rank and prerogatives of Minister. An accompanying text that spelled out his duties qualified him as "the Auxiliary of Administration". One of his main duties was to grace official events with his distinguished royal presence. The compensation for all other persons was also on these lines for it is popularly said: "If you help me scratch the rashes on my back, I will also help you when your back is itching."

At a Cabinet meeting, the Minister of Justice was assigned the task of preparing a constitution to govern the land and give government a sense of direction. This he did, but what he finally produced was a sketchy, dry document that merely stated the internal rules and regulations for Kutuma Republic. A classical constitution was still necessary, but since the Head of State measured his administration as he judged fit, state management went on according to his whims and caprices and the whole idea of a guiding constitution never resurfaced.

Running the state like a family affair did not require many written documents. When there were detractors of any kind, the Head of State called a cabinet meeting and scolded whoever had erred. Apologies were made or punishments meted out to culprits without much consideration of a constitution. Utum Tar ruled his country just like a good family head. He fed the hungry to satisfaction, and quenched the thirst of those with throats burning for alcohol. There was food and drink enough for all. This earned him such intimate names as "Baba", "father of the Nation", "saviour", amongst many others. He had become a new monarch who was revered even by the traditional paramount who had blessed him when he was setting out to the U.N. It is interesting how new power can gain prominence over the ancient one. Our people say that you make a mask, but when you give it much power it beats you.

The philosophy of "scratch my back, I scratch yours" would be the underlying principle for the one and indivisible ruling party, the Kutuma United Party, which was hastily put in place. This political creation was fashionable for a state could not function without a political party. All other countries were ruled through parties, and Kutuma was not going to be the exception. To join the dance of new independent nations, Kutuma was thus prepared in all its aspects. The party had the responsibility to glorify the initiatives of government. It was like a Ministry of Advertisement on state undertakings. If the president did one good thing, in party meetings it was announced that he had done ten. Every good undertaking had a multiplier effect.

The state and the party were just like an object and its reflection in a mirror. When state matters were concerned Tar officiated as the president and when party issues came up Tar officiated as its leader. There were slight differences of embroidery in honours; as head of state, he was referred to as "His Excellency" while on party issues he was simply "Comrade Utum Tar".

The foundation of the ruling party was a big trade fair for oratory. This was comrade Utum Tar's first public event and, to liberate himself from the powers of the *Fon*, he organized this event at the market place. By order of protocol, it was now the *Fon* who, in secondary position, arrived first to sit and wait for the president. Another set of by-laws just like those for the state had been drafted earlier. They highlighted the fact that the president of the republic would equally be the chairman of the party and that every other post in the party would be nominated at the discretion of the chairman for the sake of stability. The launching, therefore, was the reading out of these prescriptions. This was followed by volumes of speeches from convinced militants hoping for appointment. Every speech enjoyed the luxury of applause as if commanded by a choir conductor.

One year after the foundation of the state, the first ever twin presidential and legislative elections were held. Just like the formalities on the first days of the state, these elections came and went without any hitches. There were no challenges to appointed candidates. The incumbent, President Utum Tar, was the lone candidate for the presidency. The parliamentary list of 25 persons was purely a presidential appointment. One would wonder why such a wasteful event was ever held because at the close of the polls, even before counting was over, results varying between 100% and 99.99 % were being reported from every end of the Republic.

Parliament, the government and the party were three in one. They were a trinity whose mystery was the beginning and the end. The stage for the Republic had been set and the actors entered in turns.

Chapter Four

President Utum Tar loved power and knew all the tricks in the world to keep it. The state was his personal firm that had to be protected at all cost. Threats to political stability were like threats to the President's own health and had to be dealt with accordingly. For this reason, he put in place all available mechanisms to check any ambition which verged on destabilisation.

The first and most important instrument to keep his power intact was the army. Structurally, he was the head of the armed forces, though he did not know where or how to pull a trigger. He could appoint or sack anyone in the army, from General to soldier of the rank and file. But the army was not only held in control through high-handedness. He also knew that he had to pamper his "BOYS" with good salaries. No one knew from where he had his inspirations, for as a mission school teacher he had never known a luxurious salary. With a very meagre earning, he had spent his life measuring every financial undertaking with a ruler and teaspoon. That was life in the past. Now he was Head of State and lived in abundance. His world view had changed, and so he understood why every army officer needed to live well. He thus made it possible for the youngest officer to be able to ride a Renault 12 car, the cheapest at the time. He provided them with loan facilities for the purpose.. Yet most soldiers spent this money on drinking and never bought a car. Some knew very well that buying the car was one problem but running it was a greater one. Those who really bought the cars used them for clandestine transportation during their idle moments. There were many such moments because there was peace in the country. The daily routine of a soldier was simple: rise up early, go to morning assembly, execute some brisk orders from command in military jargon, march around, do some jogging and close for the day. With this straightjacket routine, most of the army officers easily grew out of shape and lost the physical fitness required by the profession. Some of the elderly ones, who had taken to drinking heavily, had developed pot bellies as indicators of affluence. Such 'pregnancies' were a common sight amongst most state workers in general because, with the growth of brewery industries in independent Kutuma, drinking was embraced by the indigenous culture. The famous prestige beer known as Gold Harp was heavily consumed, which resulted in the acronym "Government Officers like Drinking Heavily after Receiving Payment." The Kutuma soldiers drank to ascertain the veracity of this abbreviation.

Many people joined the army or police without even elementary literacy. The story goes that an illiterate police officer asked a school teacher for his identification paper. The latter presented his identity card with his photograph affixed on it. Unfortunately for the illiterate police officer, the teacher had taken this picture when he was wearing a beard. Now that he was closely shaven, the policeman argued that this was not the same person. He argued that this bushy picture did not resemble the person in front of him. All attempts to convince him to read the name and compare it with that on other identification papers fell on deaf ears. When he realized that he was being ridiculed for illiteracy, he gave the school teacher a detention for one day! The fear of the police in those days was the beginning of wisdom.

Knowing that the army was so important for state stability, recruitment was carefully scrutinized. Most of the recruits were from the president's tribal area. Some could neither read nor write. The most important tests were physical fitness and loyalty. However, for the sake of regional balance, a few recruits were handpicked from the other tribal areas of Kutuma Republic.

Another sister strategic department for monitoring power was the secret police. These were plain clothes security officers, whose role was to gather any information about activities that could threaten the peace of the state. They had many tricks for carrying out their tasks. They usually went about with small portable radio-tape recorders. They would visit off-licenses, as liquor drinking businesses were called. Here they would, unnoticed, record people's voices and take the recordings back to their offices for analysis. The secret police could provoke people to talking in exciting places like off-licenses, by introducing sensitive political topics.. Sometimes these police agents visited the homes of suspected non-conformists late at night and eavesdropped at their windows. If the victim said anything nasty about the Head of State, believing that he was in strict family confidentiality within the inner bowl of his bedroom, he never knew that there were uninvited guest lurking in the darkness outside. There were thus all sorts of strategies for information gathering. Most of the people recruited to this department shared some common characteristics. They generally appeared drunk and acted disorderly. They were noisy and provocative. In fact it was believed that they learned these skills during their training.

After collecting information, they would retire to their offices to determine how to exploit whatever they had recorded. If they found anything useful (i.e. that could be associated with destabilization), they would summon their victims for questioning. Many people were really embarrassed when they came and heard their recorded calumnious declarations. Some were judged in a military tribunal and sentenced to life imprisonment. Others were simply executed outright.

The National Radio helped greatly to strengthen the regime. This was a praise-singing organ of the state. Whenever the president made a speech, special journalists enhanced its meaning. They clearly read the speeches before they were delivered to the nation because, seconds after live broadcasts, they would provide volumes of commentary, saying what the president had said and left unsaid. These fore-runners of information shaped the mentalities of Kutumians, giving everyone the same vision and line of reasoning, all tilted towards bowing in reverence to the Great Utum Tar.

Victims of political suspicion who returned alive from the secret police investigation told listeners of the horrible ordeals to which they had been subjected. Sometime the secret police threw ground pepper into the victim's eyes and rubbed it into his nostrils and other tender parts of the body such as the armpit and sex organs. If the victim still did not speak,, he was beaten into unconsciousness where he might utter out his emotions even from the subconscious. Those charged with the torture service were well-fed and muscular enough to usually achieve the desired results.

The few dreamers who fell into this trap and were used as public examples were not really politically ambitious people considering a coup. Rather these were innocent victims who, out of sheer garrulity and drunkenness, uttered feelings of envy about the Head of State. Their treatment was usually so heavy-handed and dramatic that it served as a lesson to the rest of the country. And so life went on smoothly, with few or no persons thinking of change.

The Party was the president's magic wand. It was unofficially the sixth Ministerial Department. Its Secretary

General had the same rank and prerogatives as a minister and enjoyed a higher state budget than some ministries. The Party had Directors, Chief of Services and all the structures that existed in the conventional ministries.

The party functioned as the propaganda arm of government, disseminating to the grassroots information about governmental undertakings. It had to prepare for elections, making sure that the result ranged from 99% to 100% as had always been the case in previous elections. The party was the rallying force of the nation. Top business personalities, civil servants, traditional rulers and all who mattered tried to identify with the party as a way of showing their solidarity with the Head of State. For a civil servant to have any meaningful appointment, he needed to be an ardent militant. A businessman who wanted to enjoy tax exemption or evade an expensive tax needed to show unflinching support for the Head of State through the party. It was the gateway to success in Kutuma Republic.

Chapter Five

The army, the police, the party and all the other agents of political power played their roles, each in its own sphere. Yet the mighty chief knew he was not to live like a woman. He had to be a man by Kutumian standards, implying that he needed protection from strong *mungang* or Medicine men. Thus he did not take things lightly. At well-chosen, discrete moments, he would disappear deep in the night into the hinterlands of the Republic to consult the most renowned *mungang* men.

There was one named Bebin Bulawa who was believed to be the greatest seer of all times. He had a hidden talent that was said to be inborn. He could cause blood to flow from his eyes when he predicted something evil. This marvelled everyone. He could pull out strange objects from the body, living or lifeless. His main tool of divination was a calabash full of spring water. In the reflection of this water, he saw everything that he prophesied. It was his temple that the President visited in order to take the temperature of the state.

"As I told you earlier, your power is intact and you need only to protect it. You can pass through a raging flame and come out unscathed. But I have seen a dark cloud forming over the country," Bebin started.

"What is this cloud Bebin?" the President asked.

"This cloud is in some people's minds. It is being pushed into your country by a sweeping, wild wind blowing from other parts of the world. Just like a splinter from a bitter plant can cause very sweet wine to turn bitter, this wind is coming to upset things in your country," he further explained.

"May I know more about this threat to my peace?" his Excellency further inquired.

"There are some people who want to caress the lion because they think they are lions too. These are people who want your chair. They are the ones who want to cause that wild wind to reach here."

"Can the army, the police and the party be of help?"

Bebin Bulawa shook his calabash, squeezed the herbs in the container, and peered thoughtfully. Then he shook his head. Tears of blood dropped from his eyes.

"The army and the police will try, but their efforts will be short-lived. The change being ushered in is coming to stay. But it will stay with you. When it comes, tell it you have enough rooms in your great compound to host it. Nothing will be lost because I will prepare you against any obstacles".

"What measures, Bebin, can we take to forestall trouble?" the President asked.

"For now, look for a black cock, a goat and a virgin's head."

These requirements were to be used under cover of darkness to provide the desired protection. But for faster action, the *wutangang* 'vaccinated' his customer, cutting deep marks into the joints with a razor blade and rubbing concoctions in the cuts. Though quite a painful exercise, the Great One was bound to bear the inconveniences in order to reap the rewards later. This was the price to pay for power, and it was just the beginning. He had already gone through such protection exercises, and was always ready to take more doses and from different medicine men. Feeling now as strong as a lion, he was ready to affront any tornado that was coming to destabilize his state. Like the *mungang* man reassured him, his roots were firm in the ground; he was that *iroko* tree that must remain after any disaster.

When he returned to the Presidency, he called his private body guard and gave him Dr Bebin's prescription. The order was to be smartly executed as a matter of top state secrecy.. After all, little assignments like the need for a virgin's head came up frequently and were carried out with expertise.

For some time, the president felt uncomfortable with the recent divination, though he had received all the necessary reinforcements. To regain his good humour, he sent for his intimate friend, Ashaba, who usually shared his emotions. They drove to a chicken parlour in what was known as the *Mamiwater* Quarters to have fun. This is the place where the president usually went for relaxation and sexual pleasures. Here one could find young women of all colours, sizes and ages. Most of the young women who came here to look for greener pastures were victims of the Kutuma social order. Some were school drop-outs, others were run-away children from irresponsible parentage, while others still were former housewives in search of an alternative to marriage.

The girls in this trade were very fast when they spotted a rich man. As the president came around, there was the usual excitement, with each girl trying as much as possible to impress the well-to-do man. They employed all tactics, either shaking or bouncing the buttocks in a spectacular way as they moved along or making eyes. Despite these excitements, on this visit he spotted Natti, a woman of irresistible appeal. She had immeasurable qualities of beauty, but she could never be satisfied with one man. Her opportunity came easily, as she was fortunate enough to serve the President's table. He ordered the "Gold Harp", a drink for big people.

The President and his friend had a great deal of fun and retired to the presidency for more serious matters.

After visiting the *wutangang* and having fun with the prettiest harlot, he still could not find fulfilment. Frequently bothered by his imagination of impending doom, he often couldn't sleep. This is when he remembered the third option for solace. Being a Christian, he hurriedly said a brief prayer, addressing God but focusing his uncontrollable thought on the *wutangang*.

Chapter Six

The disruption of peace started with a rumour. In off licenses, chicken parlours, barbing studios and among the *bayam-sellam* market women, there was the rumour that an opposition party was soon to be launched to challenge the ruling one. The leader of this party was a subject of speculation. No one could say for certain who in Kutuma could be so foolhardy as to start digging his own grave by creating a party to challenge the almighty one. Some elite pointed to a certain Dr. Umza who had gone into exile since the day president Utum Tar came to power. He was known to be an outspoken critic with such verbal diarrhoea that he could not hold back his impression on any wrong doing. He had studied in a country where people did not hide their feelings. After independence, with Utum Tar in power, he immediately understood that Kutuma was no longer the right place for him. Now, with the new wind of change blowing across the world, such people could start dreaming again. But was he the one whom the *wutangang* had foreseen in that calabash?

The police, the army and the head of the party went to work, doing their best to kill public interest in the new party but this seemed like adding fuel to the burning fire of rumour.

One day, tracts were found on the streets inviting the public to launch the National Liberation Party (N.L.P). The exact date, venue and time were specified. This made the easy for the secret police. Yet the person behind the launch was still not known.

The President organized a series of secret meetings to give out firm instructions on how to deal with suspected agents of destabilization. First, he called for a cabinet meeting where he instructed the Ministers of Defence and Finance to work over-time to bring order to the republic. Order had to reign at all cost no matter how many lives would be lost. There was an abrupt salary increase of 25% for all armed officers.

The police and the army made all the necessary arrangements to stop any gathering of two or more people in the capital. Military trucks full of armed people were positioned in all the strategic corners of the city. Special attention was paid at the mortuary, round about where the tracts had announced the launch.

While the president's people meticulously prepared to counteract the launch of the National Liberation Party (The NLP), it seemed as if God was siding with the unorganized launchers. No great meetings were held, but the large appetite brought about by curiosity kept the launch flame ablaze.

Whereas at mid-day the tracts pointed to the mortuary square north of the city, mouth-to-ear communications directed interested persons to the catholic school field at 6:00 am.

Chapter Seven

What the ruling party and the government thought was going to be a small family gathering turned out to be a trade fair. There was a mammoth crowd, unprecedented in any gathering in the history of Kutuma. Many people came out not because they were convinced about change or because they had any hatred for President Utum Tar, but because of the appetite for the unknown. Opposition was a new thing and, just for curiosity's sake, many people turned out to see what it was all about. This is how the event gained popularity.

There was drumming and dancing everywhere at the unprepared ceremonial ground. When Mr Jampassdie arrived in his tattered Land Rover, he was received with heavy applause. Sycophants blew whistles and horns while party thugs feigned beating the toes of the anxious youths crowding in to have a glimpse of the new leader.

Information about this hullabaloo got to the Presidency and military headquarters, but the leaders advised that the secret police should continue its job and wait for the appropriate moment for action. By taking this decision, the military leaders had judged that it was wise for the hawk to focus well on its prey before pouncing on it. But this delay worked in favour of the launch.

Jampassdie was not a leader who would keep a distance from his people. He was not the shepherd boy who directed his flock of cattle while sitting comfortably in his hut. That is why, against all protocol, he jumped into the crowd and shook hands with his comrades. He even embraced an old lady who was suffering from the *mbingo* disease, as leprosy was commonly called. Soon he was taken to his seat by one of the protocol officers.

The first speaker came to the rostrum and there was a cemetery silence all around.

"Comrades," he began. "The time has come for you to share in moulding the history of our country. All of you present here have already registered your names with indelible ink into the invisible book of our history for posterity. History will always remember you. We are not to stand and watch our country brought to ruin by one greedy man. That is why our leader, Great Comrade Jampassdie, has taken the initiative to invite you here so that together we can bring forth this baby known as the National Liberation Party" (N.L.P). This change is a bitter but necessary pill, which we must force down the throat of our conservative ruler, Mr Utum Tar, who thinks he shall live to oppress us forever. We, the founders of Democracy, are ready for any eventuality because we want better days ahead for our children. Democracy has come to stay even if we lose our heads."

To rehearse the name of the new party, he encouraged the crowd to repeat after him:

"The National Liberation Party."

"The National Liberation Party," the crowd chorused

"Again."

"National Liberation Party."

"NLP," he abbreviated.

"NLP," the crowd bellowed.

"NLP oyeee!"

"Oyeee!"

This brief introduction was received with cheers, drumming and dancing from the crowd. He enhanced his speech with a song. He could not sing well because he had a coarse voice, but he pleaded for any young lead singer to continue it once he got it started . It went like this:

"ABC, ABC."

"Wonderful."

"In this Kutuma, we see something,"

"Wonderful."

"Small Utum Tar, Bigger than Kutuma,"

"Wonderful."

"Things must change as from today,"

"Wonderful."

People clapped and danced more for the melody than for the message for it was a popular folk tune, which many people had learned earlier in their childhood. The melody could be fitted with any message according to the context.

Then the much awaited speaker was escorted to the podium by some voluntary, self-nominated bodyguards. The excitement could be heard, seen and felt. In the crowd, there was much jostling; short people were struggling for position, some were pushing, others were standing on their toes to catch a glimpse of the speaker.

Jampassdie then started unfolding his message.

"Kutuma Oye!" he greeted.

"Oye!" the crowd answered in unison.

"NLP Oye!"

"Oye!"

"This is the day for the second independence of Kutuma. The first was independence from colonial domination. Today we are freeing Kutuma from the tyranny of one of its own sons, a son who has grown larger and taller than the Republic. The first independence was our common struggle. Unfortunately, no sooner had we obtained independence than a monarch was enthroned and took the whole country hostage. Throughout his stay in power, there has been no development in our country. Rather poverty, misery and frustration have doubled amongst our people. He has been using all sorts of intimidating and repressive methods to succeed in his high-handed rule. Today the NLP has come to remove the veil from our faces, the cataract from our eyes, so that we can see our right to progress and equitable social justice."

This speech, pregnant with all forms of persuasive devices, went on and on, expanding on the supposed plight of his militants. At the end, he invited the crowd to join him in a song of oath-taking to remain loyal to the party that they had created that day. Everyone was invited to hold his or her right hand up while singing the tune. It went thus:

We have decided to follow NLP
We have decided to follow NLP
We have decide to follow NLP
No turning back, no turning back.

Kutuma, our Country, we love you very much
Kutuma, our Country, we love you very much
Kutuma, our Country, we love you very much.
No turning back, no turning back.
Freedom has come to stay, we thank you NLP
Freedom has come to stay, we thank you NLP
Freedom has come to stay, we thank you NLP
No turning back, no turning back.

At one end, there was a woman with a baby half-asleep on her back. She was sweating profusely from the struggle in the crowd, yet her determination to follow the event right to the end was unshakeable. At another end, there was an old lady, about 80 years old, sitting down on her buttocks because her legs could no longer carry her. She had been standing for a very long time, close to three hours.

Suddenly, there was a roar and hysteria in the middle of the crowd. All attention was turned to this new centre of attraction. Someone was lying helplessly on the ground, making vain efforts to be set free. Sitting directly on his belly with legs astride him was a young woman with very tough muscles. She was giving him very hard blows on his face. From her fury you could tell that she had an additional grudge against her victim. This is the fate usually reserved for any spy detected by the crowd. A little revolver that was discovered protruding from his side had facilitated the detection and arrest of this one was. This man had been participating in all of the activities, and behaving like any ardent militant, clapping, jumping and stepping on people's toes. But, at a certain point, the boy standing next to him felt this protruding object and became curious. Then he went ahead to feel it better with his hand and noticed that this was a revolver. He immediately raised an alarm and that was why he was brought down by Natti, the tough lady of the NLP.

"Deal with him Natti," a rustic militant shouted.

"These are the enemies of change," another added.

"He must have been sent here to assassinate our leader," a third added.

By this time, the victim was lying in a pool of his own blood, bleeding from within and without.

Information got to the military headquarters that war had started. Since independence, the army had never had a real opportunity for confrontation. Some of the military officers were out of shape owing to their own inertia, so this incident was received as an opportunity for war even though the crowd had no weapons for reprisal. The commander of the military brigade, charged with the restoration of peace, reviewed all the war tactics that he had learned in the military academy some forty years back. He looked at the map behind his rocking chair, inspected a compass, and gave some orders to the lieutenant on the field using his Walkman. All of this excitement was in readiness to confront a crowd that was not prepared for war.

Suddenly there was pandemonium as troops invaded the rally ground. Some shots were fired into the air while a fierce looking soldier, with a face like that of a gorilla, sprayed bullets into the crowd. Then he turned in the direction of Jampassdie and fired three shots straight at his chest. Surprisingly, all but one missed their target completely and the third one missed his chest but caught his leg, giving him a minor wound.

The casualties in the crowd were counted. Six people were dead, including a nursing mother. Miraculously, her baby was unscathed. The bullet seemed to have undone the wrapper that tied the baby to her back, separating the baby from its mother. The baby fell directly into the crooked hands of the leper. While every unharmed person was fleeing from the surrounding danger, Mr Yeye ran towards his wife who had been shot and was lying helplessly on the ground, struggling between life and death. She had been shot in the stomach and her intestines had splashed to the ground. He scooped them with both hands and tried refitting them into her belly. This done, he stared into her face and called her name many times, but she could not answer. After a determined effort, she tried to murmur the words "take care of the children, I have gone." Then she shut her eyes forever. Mr Yeye wept like a child. As he did this, a military officer walked up to him and ordered him to leave, hitting him on the back with the base of his gun.

The last person to leave was Fundoh, the leper, holding the crying baby firm to her chest with a half arm, while creeping with the other. As she moved away, she looked back with disdain at the heartless forces. Just a few meters away, she picked up a little flag of the NLP and stuck it to her chest close to the baby. This action was enough to defy the brutality from the forces.

At the barber's workshop that evening, commentaries went on about the macabre incidents of the day.

"This Jampassdie is a special person. The woman who gave birth to such a child as him must have done so standing," one man said.

"You are right! This is someone who is bullet proof," another replied.

"I am telling you that I have seen something strange today. I was standing close to this man and saw it all. The bullets really bounced off his body and fell to the ground."

"This is clear evidence that the bullet proof vaccine is very effective. I am sure he has one."

"This man cannot be killed easily. He shall only die after accomplishing his mission on this earth."

"I hope the butcher has learned that the will of the people is stronger than any arsenal that man has ever manufactured."

As these commentaries went on, the foreign media placed the event on headline. The world was made to know of this new era in Kutuma Republic, much to the chagrin of Utum Tar who had wished to remain famous for uneasy peace. While this was great news to these foreign stations, back at home the local praise singers gave it low-key attention. There were firm orders from the Director General of Communication that no journalist should say or write anything about the incident until instructed to do so. A few days later, the government spokesman came out with an official statement:

"Last Tuesday, some hand-picked individuals attacked our National Guards on a peace keeping patrol. They killed one security officer using a rubber gun and, for this reason, our forces were obliged to react in self-defence. In the course of this retaliation, one civilian lost her life. This unfortunate incident was caused by the inordinate ambition of some vandals claiming to be party leaders. They want to create confusion and take over power. We all know our head of state as a democratic man. He knows how much democracy to prescribe for his people and is not going to yield to pressure from such misguided citizens."

After this official position, the radio and newspapers jumped in with volumes of commentaries as usual. Each one tried as much as possible to elaborate on the official statement, doing all to preserve its nucleus.

It was clear that Jampassdie had formed his party. Change had been forcibly introduced into Kutuma Republic and it had come to stay.

Chapter Eight

When moments of political tension get to their peak, it is as if the world is coming to an end. Friends are turned into enemies. Families are fragmented. People are ready to take all kinds of risks even to the point of self-sacrifice. But since no condition is permanent, life soon returns to normal after the heat is over. Even the outrageous River Kimbi that destroys any vegetation around it after a flood regains its tranquillity soon afterwards, permitting any cripple to cross even where there is no bridge.

Just one week later, Jampassdie, the hero of the launch, found himself in a sort of political recess. He had attended to the burial of the victims of the launch and had shared in the suffering of the bereaved families.

Today he was at his farm, clearing to free his crops from grass. As he worked, he had his mind focused on the event of the previous week. He regretted not staying on to challenge the military and fall like the heroes who had dropped dead. But the thought that it was necessary for him to live on so as to continue the revolution reassured him. He had not run away like a coward, but rather had tried to sustain the revolution.

As these thoughts flashed through his mind, he heard some footsteps behind him. These days he worried about his personal security, so any strange noise like this one made him shake with fright. He turned round with his machete for self-defence.

To his greatest surprise, he was visited by the broad smile of a beautiful lady. This was comrade Natti, the brave lady who had killed the secret police officer. He replied to this smile with an even more generous one.

"How did you know I was here?" he asked.

"I was merely passing by and threw my eyes in this direction," she lied.

They both sat down on a banana stem and he put his arm round her neck.

"Thank you for the visit even if it was not planned," he went ahead. "Ever since the launch, I have been anxious to see you. Congratulations on the part you played."

"Thank you," she replied. "Also accept my congratulations for your bravery in forming our party. Our republic will never be the same again."

They recounted the event in detail, talking about the inhuman regime and their determination for change. When there was nothing more to talk about, the hand caressing her back continued in non-verbal language. Action in this case speaks louder than words, it is often said. He turned towards her, took her two soft arms, threw them round his neck and pressed his chest to hers. Thus, they started their own intimacy.

The politicians in Kutuma, not just Jampassdie, shared an instinct in common. Every politician has a hidden sore which he hides during elections in well-wrapped words. Some have as many as ten mistresses. After all, some claimed, love-making to middle age people is just a form of exercise. There were many role models in this domain among leaders of the ruling party. Every visit to the outskirts presented an opportunity to take along one or another mistress.

Natti had an interesting romantic biography. She was once the girlfriend of Bebin Samali, a night watchman with a German firm. She often visited him at his work place and on some occasions they would both have fun. One day, thieves visited the firm when the two lovers were in full activity. They successfully made away with expensive valuables without the Bebin's knowledge. When the boss came and learned of this great loss, Bebin was sacked. Having no more income to continue satisfying Natti, she abandoned him.

Then she met the security guard who was lynched at the rally. This one had a handsome pay package and everything it took to manage Natti. But he treated with many girls at the same time. There were frequent fights at his house when rival girl-friends met. But Natti had no rival for she was a man in terms of energy. At one occasion, she had two teeth plucked out of her rival's mouth and threatened to cut off the boy-friend's manhood. He threatened her with his pistol and she fled. They separated, but she kept him in bitter memory. So when she had the opportunity at the launch, she had to settle scores with the Secret Police officer. The President contacted Natti still for emotional relief when he needed some relaxation. She was everywhere in the political and romantic life of Kutuma.

Now Jampassdie, the vibrant politician, was the next catch. He had no riches, but he had the potential to be a great man in the future. She judged it necessary to invest her love in him. It was not an opportunity she would want to lose. It had come so easily. They embraced each other warmly and agreed to meet often. As Jampassdie was married, this hideout was the most convenient place for nocturnal romantic appointments.

Chapter Nine

After one busy day, Jampassdie retired home for a rest. Thirsty as ever for information, he took the national daily and glanced through it for news. He was fed-up with the printed lines which monotonously carried only obituaries and tenders for contracts. These empty papers were, however, helpful in the sense that, when he was bored and felt like glancing through them, he was easily lulled to sleep. Just as his eyelids were closing, the four battery radio placed on the side stand of his bed pulled his attention back to a sensitive news item. This was preceded by the usual news jingle and the customary hymn saluting dictatorship.

"One of our top stories tonight, presidential elections have been declared for this year. A detailed schedule will be made available in the months ahead. Meanwhile, the Head of State has signed a release authorizing six political parties to operate in our Republic. This is in keeping with his ideals of democracy."

Jampassdie jumped to his feet and pressed the radio set close to his ears. He really wanted the radio to answer the when, how, where, and why of the brief news item, but the closing jingle was already there playing. To satisfy his curiosity, he would have to wait for the praise singers to clarify the information, adding what the writer of the circular had forgotten.

This government's strategy, keeping the public in suspense over the details of the election and the list of authorized parties, was designed to take the opposition movement by surprise. After getting the reaction from the opponent movement, the government was to expand on the modalities of elections in the favour of the ruling party.

Aware of this trap, Jampassdie decided to summon his party bigwigs to a think-tank meeting. During this meeting, he elaborated a campaign strategy. Being a party for the oppressed, it was agreed that he should be very vocal on Human Rights abuses, the widespread poverty, unemployment and general misery of the populace. Every campaign speech was to highlight these weaknesses of the government in power. Since this was the first presidential election organized since the advent of multi-party politics in Kutuma, the NLP was determined to take the bull by its horns. For twenty-four years, the president had cunningly refused to organise elections.

When the meeting started, Jampassdie introduced its purpose, emphasizing the need for the opposition to be disciplined and sharply focused to confront the coming challenge. He called on his collaborators to come up with strategies to counteract any form of vote rigging.

Before he could finish talking, Mr Ngam raised his finger and comrade Jampassdie offered him the floor. Mr Ngam was clearly anxious and had raised this finger at least three times while Jampassdie was speaking. Mr Ngam spoke:

"Comrades, I know we have very eloquent people among us. We do not lack words. But we need to take important decisions now. We should decide on our candidate or candidates for the post of President. Let us try to open a new page of democracy instead of treading on the footsteps of the crumbling reign."

There was an excited reaction to that point. The most vocal and sentimental reaction was from comrade Natti:

"We all know the man who ventured into the lion's den at the launch. This man, who exposed his head to the butcher, should not be doubted as our lone candidate. Let us, therefore, not belabour the point. We have our God-given leader, the brave comrade Jampassdie." Quite confident and satisfied with the weight of the point, she took back her seat

Another speaker jumped up and blasted at Bebin Ngam and nicknamed him "the enemy in the house." How could he have brought up such a point? This position, daring to propose a rival to Jampassdie, was one that could set fire in the party. So far the opposition was one and indivisible; any attempt to depart from its initial goals was tantamount to destabilisation. He even insisted that militants like Bebin Ngam might have been planted by the ruling party in an attempt to fragment and weaken the opposition.

Yet Bebin Ngam was not alone in his position. Controversy is like wine; the thirst increases with an additional cup, so arguments developed with new ideas. The proper measure for democracy lies in the voting. Supporters of comrade Jampassdie did not see any reason to waste time with an election on the matter. Bebin Ngam also had his followers. Comrade Freeboy got up and backed the contestants requesting that the issue be put to vote. Some argued, with cloudy logic, that the post of president should be reserved for the founding fathers of the party. The brave people who had launched the party needed to be protected. Their courage was to be considered a life investment, and adventurers should not be permitted to replace them in the course of the political journey.

This is when many people saw that the constitution of the party was very shallow. It had not foreseen such controversial issues. But these lapses were not unique to the National Liberation Party. Even the constitution of the Republic of Kutuma was never handled with any seriousness, and Utum Tar enjoyed it as it was since he could always alter one clause or another to suit his machinations to conserve his power.

In the end, the debates of the day were a total fiasco with no resolution on the issue of candidature. At the close of the meeting, there were two camps of equal strength on the matter. The meeting ended with everyone talking angrily at the same time. Even comrade Nduchum, the pastor, could not call the assembly to order for prayers.

Chapter Ten

Politics is like a game of football. When the careless player stands with his legs astride, the fast dribbler sends the ball between his legs, obtaining swift advantage. He gives the opponent an applauded *nzolo* as it is known in common parlance. Utum Tar was a fast dribbler. He understood from all secret police sources that the opposition was already swimming in troubled waters, and he prepared to take fast advantage of their disunity.

To this effect, he summoned an emergency caucus meeting of the ruling party. This was a meeting for the men and women of timbre and calibre, whose physical appearances announced their seriousness. Most of the militants alighted from expensive cars, great symbol of status. To youth, these people were role models of fashion. But when one peeped closer into the lives of such models, it could be noticed that half of their relations had died in the most abhorrent of manners, that some of them made love with their comrades of the same sex, and that many put the nation's wealth into their pockets, which were as deep as an abyss. There were untold hidden agendas behind those glittering cars. Each of the participants was hefty, juicy and sweet smelling. These were the president's men and women, and he counted on them for his prolonged stay in power.

Outside the meeting hall, there were highly animated cultural dances from across the length and breadth of the country. Remarkably, some of the dancers had also danced at the opposition rally. But now they were ardent followers of the ruling party. Double standards were common in Kutuma politics. Those who took particular advantage to double deal were the jujus, not because they wore masks and could not be identified as crossing the carpet, but because they were a necessary feature for cultural animation in Kutuma life. At the opposition rallies, they danced for the joy of dancing; at the ruling party meetings, they danced to obtain bright bank notes from the ventilated pockets of juicy militants.

The meeting started with an all too familiar melody in praise of the achievements of the Great One. The lead singer was Comrade Ngon, one of the latest catches from the *'Mamiwater'* Quarters of the chicken parlours where big people went for relaxation. This is a lady who started a business with two crates of drinks, but now went abroad to Dubai to import special lady fashion designs. She had grown very rapidly in business, thanks to her bottom power. At the close of her song, she reminded the assembly of the answer to the responsorial psalm of the day, which went thus:

Call Phrase: President Utum Tar!
Answer: President for life.
Call Phrase: President Utum Tar!
Answer: President for life
Call Phrase: President Utum Tar!
Answer: Our unique candidate.

When she sat down, drenched in her own sweat from face and armpits, she was saluted with deafening and prolonged applause. The other speeches that followed this prologue were merely extensions of that carefully planned theme. As she took her seat at the executive table, it was now the time for President Tar to talk. He preceded all his speeches with a commanding cough. Many thought he was clearing his throat.

"I have heard your clarion call for me to stay in power. I have read the many motions of support addressed to me on this subject. Committed to the defence of our national peace and development, which together we have fostered since independence, I do so swear that I will not disappoint your wishes."

There was applause.

"But we must be careful because times have changed. Whether by design or chance, an evil spirit has visited our home in the name of democracy. This new notion permits the goat to invite the lion boxing, knowing fully well that one is food for the other. With this disturbing turn of events, we must not sit on our laurels. Let us prepare for any new surprises. I will soon be sending out campaigns teams. Let us confirm our popularity through the ballot box. This means that we will need to use the force of argument to win everyone to our side, not the argument of force."

This point was again saluted with deafening applause.

"We have established more political parties because we stand to gain from a pluralistic set-up. But I want to warn those who think that they can bite the finger that feeds them. Political pluralism does not mean anarchy. In this new game, I will not tolerate anyone who tries to disturb our national peace for his personal greed for power."

"As elections are coming up, let the ruling party demonstrate its maturity. Let us prove that we are the oldest, the strongest and the most popular. Let it enter the annals of history that we have embraced democracy and done it better than those who introduced it to us." (Applause)

Like any good politician, these words were eloquent, but they sounded from without and not from within.

After this talk, the meeting came to a close to the satisfaction of the militants.

The radio expanded on this speech, giving President Utum Tar such honorific names as "the father of transparency." His selflessness, they hailed, had given room for others to create new parties. There could hardly be a replacement for such a great ruler. It was time for the people of Kutuma to make the right choice. There was only one divine choice. This is how the press organ of the party summed up the campaign speech.

As the president moved home, he was saluted with energetic dance displays. Some flashy bank notes were dished out as usual to the dance groups. Such notes could send the dancers into frenzy. The lead dancer, or the *Kam*, would dash into the air and alight on tiptoe and then go on his knees for more notes to be pasted on his mask.

That evening, the radio sang the praise song and opened campaigns for the ruling party well ahead of time.

No one doubted that the ruling party would win. Whoever wanted to participate ought to know that the host country with home advantage was poised to win. The referees and all stakeholders were supposed to know this well. The president had the yam, the knife and the mouth.

Chapter Eleven

After the war of words at the National Liberation Party think-tank meeting, Bebin Ngam did not take things lying down. He was ready to drive his point through and through. With full knowledge that Jampassdie was fast becoming another Utum Tar, he had decided to come out with the progressive wing of the National Liberation Party. He had come to understand that change in the political dance was just like one dancer taking off his mask to wear another one and appear different. Bebin Ngam was not ready to see Jampassdie grow into a giant, eclipsing everyone else.

But this had not been his original idea. He had been motivated by the President's men, who had been paying him constant nocturnal visits to prompt him into this new way of thinking. They usually came along with suit cases loaded with shiny, virgin bank notes.

"You are not obliged to spend all of your life blowing Jampassdie's trumpet," they would advise him. "It is high time you try to project your own image. You should take your destiny into your own hands. As a political leader, you enjoy a stronger charisma than him. The head of state has seen your potential and takes you more seriously." This bait of words was accompanied during the last visit by a handsome envelop, containing two million Frs. To add to this, he was promised the post of Deputy Director of the Treasury, a post which was never given to anyone except the president's men of confidence.

Being a pragmatic man, Bebin Ngam, accepted these offers wholeheartedly. He was not idealistic. He saw politics as a business built on direct interest. No matter how good and genuine an ideological position was, it fell short of expectations when it did not provide food for its defenders. No woman would till a farm, knowing that in the end there would be no yield; that would be sheer waste of energy.

After the meeting, he retired to his Kilofi quarters with the determination to make amends. But it was not as easy as he had imagined. Managing a break away was not as easy as eating a bowl of *fufu* or enjoying a bottle of Kutuma beer. The first challenge he faced was establishing a following in his vicinity, a little quarter that could be taken for his stronghold, having only three compounds, all belonging to his relatives. Bebin Ngam, the Man of substance, was equal to whatever challenges would arise. Since he was on the popular side, working for the ruling party, the media were ready to help him rally the public

Beyond the media tactic, Bebin Ngam developed another formula to get more people to his rally. With the handsome packet that he had received, it was possible for him to turn the tables by any means. He came up with a wonderful idea for bait: food and drink. This was a clever stratagem in a culture where consciences were governed by such values. To this effect, he had bought an elephant-sized bull, and when the animal was brought and tethered at the entrance into his compound, all passers-by commented on the awaited "item eleven". A bull in Kilofi, a cattle grazing area, was no big deal as its price was quite affordable. This permitted the Bebin to offer a feast of generosity unprecedented in recent times in the village. People ate before, during and after the rally and there were still leftovers. Before the day of his party's launch, his wives had prepared many pots of corn beer, enough to keep the whole village in a festive mood throughout the period.

When all was set, the population started assembling. The first hour was quite quiet .It seemed as if everyone was looking at his next neighbour to take the lead in betraying the initial ideals set collectively upon the launching of the original NLP. Now appetite for the bull was more salivating than that first emotional anxiety. As time went on, the assembly grew larger and larger. Soon there was no available sitting space. Most people stood where they could enjoy the awaited meal. What seemed most intriguing was that some of the hard-core members of the main party were in attendance. Even comrade Natti, who had taken a very active part in launching the original party, was present. A remarkable feature of the event was that it was more about feasting than speech-making. Here action mattered, not words.

As formality requires, Bebin had to welcome his guests at the start of business. Standing majestically at his doorsteps with airs of the well-to-do, he went ahead:

"Dear militants, advocates of real democracy, thank you all for honouring my distress call. This is the moment of the truth. Yesterday we were all on one path. But when I noticed that one big elephant was going to swallow us and take us hostage, I decided to trace a new path away from his tusks. We are now the progressive wing of the National Liberation Party. But we are not a separate entity. We shall never leave the National Liberation Party because we fought for it, together with those who now want to destroy it. What we want to guard against is the one-man dictatorship of Mr Jampassdie. We are ready to fight it right to the energy of the last man without surrendering. Long live positive thinking, long live democracy, and long live the Republic of Kutuma."

The speech was as brief as the man, for Bebin Ngam was a man of slight build. He had preached his truth, but the time for real truth was soon to ring. The truth now started coming out in large drums of beer and basins of corn *fufu* loaves and pots of stew.

The public clown known as Young Boy offered the audience small doses of his characteristic humour. He was well over eighty, but looked like a boy of twelve. What betrayed him was his grey hair; otherwise he could be mistaken for a teenager. He often told people that the secret behind his unchanging youth was a life of humour. He saw the world as a garden, flowering with jokes. When he had an event of merry-making like today, he took advantage of the circumstance to thrill his audience with the life-extending drug of humour.

"As Young Boy is smacking his lips and crushing that last tendon, I know that he will soon hit us with a joke," someone prompted.

"No, his stream of jokes is dry. Heavy eating has emptied his stock," another one chimed in.

"You people should not disturb a bachelor who has a rare opportunity to enjoy well-cooked corn *fufu* from a woman," said Young Boy.

"How can you refer to yourself as a bachelor when we all know that you are the proprietor of all the available women in this village?" a third voice added.

"They are not available to me only. They are mine in daylight but under cover of darkness they belong to all of you who are all now pretending to be so saintly," Young Boy defended himself.

"Is that all you have for us today as joke, Young Boy?"

"No," he replied sharply. "Permit me to describe you, for you look like a good juicy Minister of the Government in power. When did you come back from the white man's country?" Young Boy embarrassed him in his characteristic style.

"What could I have gone there for?" the man retorted.

"He is asking me, ooo! Is it not said that all big men go there when they feel wrinkled? Are we not told that they go there to change their blood and grow younger? That their bodies are like calabashes frequently emptied and refilled? That when they get there, the old worn out blood is drained out and replaced with fresh young blood? Today you see them old and wrinkled, but tomorrow you meet them and they have a formidable youthful radiance. That is the rich man's formula for staying young, a really expensive one. It works only for those who have the money to spend, who can afford to pay the transport service of a metallic bird to fly out of Kutuma. You people ought to understand that I am doing you a lot of good with my free youth-extending drugs. How many of you ever care to show me gratitude, you ungrateful lots of Kutuma?"

The audience responded with laughter at this strange humour, even though many doubted the practicality of this clinical exercise. The local folk could not make much sense of this joke about emptying and refilling blood in a human being, though Young Boy had elaborated very eloquently on the practice.

The audience went wild with laughter. Another prompter cut in when the excitement lowered.

"But Young Boy, can you tell us why you have remained a bachelor all through your life? Do all these charming, beautiful young women not appeal to you?" he asked.

"There you go again," Young Boy answered, smiling cynically. "For all the years I have lived on this earth I have never come across a single beautiful young woman. When I meet one with a fair complexion, I am disappointed with her legs, which look like roasted yams as a result of extravagant lotions. The one who is full-breasted has no rounded backyard; then the seemingly perfect one, with strikingly attractive features, lacks a warm heart. I hope you are satisfied with these answers. You may also like to know that I have not given up hope, especially now that modern trends have brought in additional dimensions to what we call marriage. The market for women is dying out as men are getting married to men. As a permanent young man, I will go for the sweetest looking young boy of this quarter. Are you happy with my Bachelorhood now that it is soon coming to an end?" he said, sneezing.

"God forbid Young Boy!" Someone cut in. "If you are the one to introduce man-to-man relationships in our village, we will lynch you. We don't want to hear of such an abomination. May it end with those who started it. For what pleasures can a man find in another man's buttocks? Do we want the world to come to an end? No, God forbid!"

The audience responded with laughter, even though many doubted the veracity of the idea of men getting married to men. Young Boy could hold the audience's attention for hours with many such strange stories without their tiring.

When the entertainment was over, there was the usual bustling atmosphere of traditional dances. Right in the centre of the ring, wriggling her waist in frenzy, was comrade Natti. Bebin Ngam came round in his flowing gown and placed a shiny bank note on her forehead. This seemed enough to transport her heart completely into the event. The note could be the introduction to a romantic feeling afterwards, for Natti never offered any objection to persons of high calibre. While her group entertained this way, the jujus did so the other way.

As evening approached, the excitement died down and the population dispersed.

The radio sang about the event, glorifying the new hero and giving a pejorative picture of Jampassdie. Yet this glorification was limited to ensure that the new hero should not grow taller than Great Utum Tar. A tributary can never be greater than a river; neither can the shoulder be higher than the head.

Chapter Twelve

Campaign fever got to its peak on the last market day of Ndindi village. Jampassdie was prepared for campaigns and ready to fight against all odds. This was his political stronghold and he had decided to hold his campaign rally there. The people of Ndindi had a religious attachment to the ideals of the National Liberation Party.

When the market was full to the brim, the crowd swaying this way and that way, the village usher got to the rock, which served as a podium, and made the usual call for order:

"Ooooooooo market, listen!" he shouted.

"Ooooooooo market, listen!"

He was carrying the traditional *Kwifon* spear, meaning that he was addressing the public with the authority of the *Fon*; so everyone was bound to respect the order.

In modern times, when few persons gave gifts to the *Fon*, he got revenue for the running of the palace by using the spear at ceremonies. Every politician who needed *Kwifon's* intervention went and gave a token to invite the usher. This is what Jampassdie had done. After obtaining independence, and with the passing of time, President Utum Tar had neglected the *Fon*. That function of Auxiliary of Administration had been dropped with repeated cabinet shake-ups. With little sources of income, the *Fon* had realized that he could, in a multi-party system, make money during rallies using the spear. Any political party that needed this instrument of discipline, to run its rally, went to the palace to obtain the Fon's authorisation; this is what Jampassdie did on this day.

After this call to order, Mr Jampassdie mounted on the natural stage.

Today, he was at the apex of his inspiration. Knowing the frustrations of his people, he touched on key issues that could move even very cold people to exhilaration. Generally, he never prepared his speeches, but when he mounted the pulpit he spoke like one reading from a written script.

"Fellow Kutumians, the election day is just a few hours away when everyone is going to free himself or herself from the bondage of the tyrant. Through the ballot box, you decide the future of the nation. Ask yourselves why we all pay taxes to run the state, yet the treasury of the land is in the hands of a privileged few. Why is it that the sun is shining on all of us, yet some people think that they can lock us up in darkness, so that the rays cannot touch us? Our president is preaching democracy and has given the word a special definition of his own. In his understanding, democracy is in his pocket; it is like grains of groundnuts in his pockets. From time to time, he brings out a few grains to give us, treating Kutumians like little, crying babies who can be tricked with a few grains of democracy. He throws the last grains into his mouth. We are on the eve of elections, yet more and more political parties are being created. This is a trick to derail our attention. Beware of these new false prophets who will be claiming to take you to glory land, which is nothing short of the tyrant's dungeon. These are the multiple voices of the king, for they are all at his service. Some of our militants have fallen prey to the temptation of the tyrant's bank notes. Know that this is temporary salvation. Our party remains one and indivisible. There is nothing like a progressive wing of the N.L.P. This divisive strategy, put in place by one of us, is just an idle thought, motivated by the corrupt regime and facilitated by greed.

Its agents are already out with packets of shiny notes to share with you, to buy over your consciences. When they come, take the money because it is the tax payer's money. But remember to hold tight to your good conscience. After all, how can someone use your own money to buy favours from you?

When I talk about the tax payers' money, you all understand the torture that our taxation policy subjects us to. Even an old mother, who cannot meet her survival needs, pays tax. I know that if this regime continues to rule, it won't be long before you are taxed for defecating. This is a fact. You are all paying for water and light, and you will soon pay for oxygen and your own stool."

There was applause and drumming. Then he continued.

"Fellow comrades, our frustrations caused by the present regime are legion. I have summed them up as 99 points against the tyrant, but for want of time I will talk only about the top nine.

Point One: Embezzlement

There are some people in this country whose private wealth can run the republic for decades. They have used their high offices to embezzle more than their families will be able to exhaust for many generations. Greed has blinded some of our compatriots to the extent that they are not concerned about the plight of others. Let us correct this ill through the ballot box.

Point Two: Poverty

While some swim in affluence, the majority live in abject poverty. Most of our citizens cannot fend for themselves. Were it not for our agriculture, most of us would have starved to death. Many people who cannot afford the cost of medication die without going to the health centre.

Point Three: Tribalism and Marginalisation

Is there a man who is less than a man because of his size? The Utum Tar regime has decided that it should be so in

Kutuma. Here it has been decreed that one tribe should govern while others should be governed. We do not need to question God for creating some people and placing them in the minority tribe. We have only the god of Kutuma to blame, for it is he who thinks that belonging to the minority is a curse. I have the conviction that all of you, comrades of sound judgement, irrespective of your tribe of origin, shall sanction this injustice come Election Day.

Point Four: Bribery

Where is the place of merit in our society? Mediocrity has overthrown excellence in a wrestling duel refereed by Utum Tar. Appointments go mostly to less qualified persons who have pocket power. Competitive exams are treated the same way. Men need pocket power, while women do it with bottom power. That is the practice. This tradition must change through our collective decision on Election Day.

Point Five: Underdevelopment

We have refused to receive civilization by keeping in power people who believe that underdevelopment is part of our cultural heritage. In an age when people in other parts of the world ride cars on good roads, haves telephones and the essentials of life like electricity and water, when modernity has made life worth living, the majority of Kutuma has been deprived by his own selfish and greedy brother in power. Lend us your trust and we will deliver the goods.

Point Six: Human Rights Abuse

What is left of a man when he cannot express his feelings? On several occasions, the man of Kutuma has been crushed by bullets because he attempted to express his opinion. When the gun is not used, he is locked up in a police cell under very uncomfortable conditions. The abbreviation, KUP, says it all. KUP stands for Kutuma Under Pressure. The National Liberation Party is the answer to the rule of terror. We are here to liberate the nation from tyranny. Give us a chance and life in Kutuma will never be the same again.

Point Seven: Inertia in the Administration

Our public offices offer maximum torture to its users. It is common to go to an office and find only coats hanging on chairs while the workers are idling about. Some people actually leave those coats there and return home for private purposes. They only come back to the office at closing time to collect their coats and shut their doors and windows. When they are blamed for this nonchalance, some say, "What is important is joining the civil service and getting into the pay roll of the state, not the work." The National Liberation Party intends to turn a new page in the administration of Kutuma.

Point Eight: Monopoly

In a State like ours where monopoly is the order of the day, how can we expect democratic expression? We have only one radio station, one company that provides electricity, one that is in charge of the water supply. Apart from the multiplicity of political parties and churches, all public utilities have no alternative. You either take what the monopoly master offers you or you perish. We are all taken hostage by this regime .Let us reverse the situation through the upcoming elections.

Point Nine: Unemployment

The youth of our country has been sacrificed. Countless qualified graduates are roaming the streets with no jobs. The odd practice, dear comrades, is that grandfathers who are overdue for retirement cling to their offices, occupying positions that could be handed to their young ones. How can the situation ever change if this regime remains in power? I know of a paradoxical situation in one ministry where a son has gone on retirement before his father. This is possible only in Kutuma, a country notorious for the negative reversal of roles. A vote for the National Liberation Party will be the start of the solution to this aching problem."

A thunderous applause saluted these embarrassing realities.

While most of the listeners reacted with enthusiasm to these words, somewhere in isolation, Bebin Chiatoh listened with the utmost scepticism. The latter, an uncle of Jampassdie, had been ostracised with the allegation that he belonged to a secret cult known as *Famla*. When anyone died in the family, all was blamed on Bebin Chiatoh. It is said that he got into this cult and negotiated to sell as many as a hundred people mystically. Jampassdie also believed this. He had recently been warned by a *wutangang* that he would soon be a victim. Though this believe was popular, there was no visible sign of riches in the Bebin. He even lived in a grass thatched house and owned very little property. With the outbreak of AIDS, many people gave credence to the belief that Bebin was finishing the family, and even Jampassdie alluded to him at his rally as an undesirable member. That is why Bebin Chiatoh could never take anything Jampassdie said without a pinch of salt.

Then Jampassdie shifted his talk from blame to promises.

"When you permit me to run the affairs of our fatherland, the farmer shall be a happy person forever. I will give pride of first priority to self-reliant Development and improve the agricultural sector. Not only will I create more schools of agriculture, but I will ensure that the graduates from this school are very useful to society. For too long, we have seen engineers dressed in suits and going to sit on rocking chairs in offices. That practice must end. We need engineers who are in the field, guiding our farmers. We are breaking into a new dawn when you shall no longer be duped of your produce. You shall have opportunities to market your goods directly to the world market. This will encourage us to farm not only for subsistence but for serious economic empowerment. We are already a blessed people because we have what the white man envies. We have abundance of land and that is our wealth. We will be able to boastfully say that we are the bread basket of the world if we develop our agriculture. The future is undoubtedly bright for the farmer if you make the right choice come Election Day." He made this pronouncement with a lot of authority since he was himself a farmer.

"I have a plan for everyone in our country. But I can't cover it all within so short a time. Permit me to sum up with a short message to the civil servants. The follow up of individual files for promotion will be an issue of the past. I will not be a head of state who signs decrees without texts of application. It is scandalous to find people who, after working for twenty years, have the same salary scale as when they started. As soon as I take over office, the yearly assessment sheet, signed by your immediate boss, will be directly considered for increment."

Pa Jato, listening to the speech, nodded with approval at this for, as a classroom teacher, he had taught for twenty eight years with no promotion because he had no Godfather. The society had functioned on the rule of benevolent gods who could give you a post if you fulfilled certain conditions. Only the privileged ones, those who had brothers on the treetops, were allowed to eat ripe fruit. Those who had no brothers on tree tops needed to trace their paths to high offices with heavy sums of money.

When he gave the usual call formula at the end of his campaign speech, the response was as heavy as on launch day. It was as reassuring as he could make it. The opposition had apparently grown stronger and was prepared to affront any adversaries come Election Day. Today he rounded off with a tune of hope, indicating that victory was close at hand:

> *Tune: our party wins the game*
> *Chorus: ewa*
> *Tune: NLP wins the game*
> *Chorus: ewa*
> *Tune: oppression dies today*
> *Chorus: ewa*
> *Tune: change has come to stay*
> *Chorus: ewa*
> *Tune: our party wins the game*
> *Chorus: EEE wins the game, ewa*

Normal activities resumed in the market shortly after the political rally. The deep hum of the crowd could be heard even kilometres away. The population on this particular *Fukehi* market day was immense because news had gone round about the opposition party rally.

Beyond economic considerations, a market day was an opportunity for social interaction. People came out to meet one another, shake hands, get news from various corners of the village and, above all, eat and drink. In short, it is said in the Ndindi language that people go to the market to 'eat'.

This merry-making was soon interrupted by an incident. Moses Maan, a member of the break-away faction of the N.L.P., had left his house that morning with the determination to disrupt Jampassdie's rally. He planned to settle scores with his lifetime enemy, Freeboy. After drinking some litres of the strong local liquor, he was armed for the assault. When he met the intended victim, without any waste of time, he spat on his face and insulted him in a highly provocative manner, using the rapped tongue that produced a '*ntrrh*' sound, like the quack of a hen. He had timed this provocation well, just when Freeboy was chatting with a girlfriend. The latter could not stomach this. To pay back provocation with provocation, Freeboy immediately cut some grass, feigned cleaning his anus with it and shot it at Moses Maan's face. To a man of Kutuma birth, this was highly provocative. Prepared for a fight, he leaped forward and the two men were soon entangled in a wrestling position. The crowd booed as is customary when there is such an incident. As the struggle went on, Moses had the upper hand. He trapped his opponent's left leg and both went down. Yet Freeboy struggled on to avoid his back from touching the ground, for in such a duel, one was defeated if his back was brought to floor level. This is when his friend jumped in to help, causing Maan to lose his grip. Soon more of Maan's and Freeboy's friends joined and there were many more pairs of wrestlers. After the wrestling, fierce boxing took over. This is when brave young men displayed their physical prowess while women and children watched and booed.

This free-for-all fight ended as abruptly as it had started, with no clear victor or vanquished. But a few people were wounded and others had torn dresses.

When normal activities resumed in the market, Chiafukun, a drunkard in one of the *'nkang'* drinking stalls, boasted that he was the architect of this display. He claimed that, before leaving his house that morning, he had prepared the fighting spell known as *'gwofukang'* to excite the public to fight. It was commonly believed that when somebody got up in the morning of a market day, burnt the *'gwofukang'* medicine, and blew its ashes in the direction of the market, there would be a fight that day. This is what Chiafukun claimed he had done, and he was very proud of his success. In this period of political tension, political differences provided the fuel for the *'gwofukang'* medicine to burn with strong effect.

As Chiafukun boasted about his powers in conjuring fighting spells, another member of the drinking club interrupted him, calling on listeners to discuss a subject of more topical interest given the pending elections. This was Mundah.

"When we come together, let us discuss one or two topics that can help us in our development. I am not here to talk about fighting. Now the question I am putting forth is whether there a real possibility of beating President Utum Tar on the 20th. What real strategies can Jampassdie or any political leader use to defeat Utum Tar?" he asked.

There was meditative silence for a while. Then Mangan broke in. "Well, I am afraid to pronounce on the matter because if I talk in favour of one party, another fight may begin. I don't have physical strength and I am left with only a few teeth for my food. I cannot withstand any blows. I can only say something if everyone is ready to be tolerant, for I can't read your minds to say who belongs to which party," he concluded.

"Please Mangan," Mundah went on. "I think we now enjoy freedom of all sorts. You are free to express yourself as you wish. The democracy we are clamouring for has come to stay. Feel free to say what you think."

This is when Young Boy the clown, who this far had been unusually quiet, said he had a suggestion. Once he started talking, people started laughing without understanding what he was saying because they knew his ideas were generally funny.

"My point is that people are wasting so much time and money to send President Utum Tar away. There is that short cut to success using the rain. I hope you understand me?" he intimated.

"What do you mean? Put your point straight," someone stepped in.

"The Bobe Yuh and the Giant Rat story is a living reality of how that method works," he continued.

"What is it about?" a prompter asked.

"That his money disappeared, a big bundle of money. Bobe Yuh suspected all the neighbours in his vicinity, even his own wives. For days and market weeks, he could not eat anything because he had borrowed this money from a *'njangi'* and had the obligation to pay it back. He became as pale as a broom stick. His youngest son felt sorry for him and told him he had had a dream that this money was not taken by someone from afar. He said that the thief lived near him. This intensified his doubt as to the honesty of his wife and children. He decided to go and see *Besingang*, the diviner. The latter confirmed and guaranteed that the money was around and could be recovered. He was asked to provide a black fowl, a blanket and some cam wood. But to proceed with the research, it was necessary to be sure that neither his wife nor his children were involved. The diviner took one name after another and verified using his amulets. Their innocence was confirmed.

With assurance doubly confirmed, the *Besingang* dispatched the black magic cock during a light drizzle. This was followed by a splash of lightening and a deafening thunder bang, 'PANGKALANGLANG!!!' which left a big crack in Bobe Yuh's compound. This crack went deep down into the dwelling of a giant rat, bringing it out dead, accompanied by the missing purse. Unfortunately, the money had been chopped in its edges and some of the bank serial codes had been destroyed. You can see that the rain method never misses its target especially when theft or indebtedness is involved.

"Mr Young Boy, your story is good for listening. But its practicability in the promotion of democratic change is doubtful. Even if we want to go by that method, does President Utum Tar owe anyone?

"Yes of course. He owes even you. He owes the entire Republic the tax payer's money."

"But the action of the Rain-Cock is counteractive. If it misses its target, it bounces back on the sender. Who would it get in the case of failure, since everyone is the sender?"

"Well, in that case, the *Besingang* would direct it into a fresh banana tree to cool down its fury.

This dream talk from Young Boy was taken as a big joke. In democracy, everyone has a right to his opinion even if it is a baseless dream. So Young Boy the clown had a right to his own opinion but no obligation to implement it.

Chapter Thirteen

As the campaign hysteria raged on, the chief executive of state, President Utum Tar, could not just sit with folded arms. He had to convene a meeting of (the Ruling Organ of) the party to map out campaign strategies. Various teams were set up and sent to electoral districts across the length and breadth of the Republic. This kept the whole state busy. Every top civil servant in the administration had to return to his land of birth to organise rallies. The Treasury provided huge sums of money for these missions. The ministers knew that the President would reorganize his cabinet after the elections and that their performance would determine their reappointment. Many of the ministers had acquired fortunes through their positions and were able to contribute extra money to the election fund to enhance their prospects. This is when those expensive all-weather four-wheel drive vehicles would be useful. The election teams came in with cartons of nice wine, bags of salt, soap, rice and many other valuables to pamper the electorate. Every neighbourhood enjoyed unusual feasting.

The team that was sent to Ndindi, Jampassdie's stronghold, was a special one as they knew this would be a hard nut to crack. It was made up of people with a religious belief in the ruling party. The right man, Minister of State Adamu Ndi, was chairman of the team. They got to Ndindi late at night after a tedious journey of pushing the car on a muddy road and found lodging in a local hotel.

These imminent personalities either brought girlfriends with them or made new ones on the spot. Minister Ndi never took anyone with him. As chance would have it, the first lady he met in Ndindi was Natti and he could not resist her charms. His body guard immediately made arrangements for the minister to have a nice night.

Then the team paid a courtesy call to the Head of Administration, the main organiser of the elections, and gave out the confidential instructions from party headquarters. These contained all the rigging manoeuvres put in place by the ruling party. The instructions were uniform all over the territory and the main one was that some ballot boxes should be stuffed well in advance with ballot papers. The Head of Administration had to fill some return sheets and fake signatures on them well ahead of counting. Then, for purposes of popularity, people could be brought in from neighbouring villages to vote twice. Most importantly, voting cards of known opposition members had to be hidden. The Head of Administration was responsible for updating the voting register right up to the morning of voting day. Most members of the ruling party were permitted to own extra cards in the names of dead relatives or people living too far from the village to come in for the vote. Before Election Day, forces of law and order were to be mobilised all over the territory to prevent rioting. After the brainstorming meeting, the minister returned to his hotel room and social matters.

The professional traditional dancers that entertained at every rally soon invaded the market arena. The same people attended the ruling and opposition party rallies. It was hard to say whether they were heeding the opposition's call to enjoy the tax payer's money or simply hanging on to the party that brought good food and nice wine. Everyone was clothed in newly printed t-shirts and fez caps bearing a picture of the Head of State, giving a real glamorous appearance to the scene. The spray of bank notes was more generous than ever before.

Before the rally could end, the opposition stole the show. What an embarrassing situation to the minister! The confidential text bearing party instructions on the rigging procedure had been pasted on the entrance to the market. Another copy had been pasted on his car. The minister stood dumbfounded. Sweat trickled down his face and he was totally drenched in perspiration. He ordered the police to do their job and scolded them for lack of vigilance. He wondered inwardly if there was a malicious hand behind this betrayal.

With frail limbs, like a convalescent, anaemic patient, he walked to his hotel room. He had locked the door and, surprisingly, it was still intact. His suit case, containing all these valuables, was neatly locked and he had taken the key with him. Who was to blame? The Head of Administration to whom he had given a copy could not have done such an insane thing. His bodyguard had served him honestly for the past five years with hardly an error and no hint of betrayal. Every person in his entourage could be trusted. But could he have the same trust in Natti, a woman he had met just a few hours earlier? That was his biggest doubt.

The opposition made a great fuss about this discovery, but the radio and all other forms of dissuasion did everything possible to cover it up. The minister said that these were tracts fabricated by the opposition to influence the public. Despite this attempt to conceal the truth about the imminent rigging, the opposition knew too well that they needed counter strategies to forestall this abuse of democratic expression. There was an antidote for every point on the rigging plan. Most importantly, the population needed to come out during the counting exercise to watch for and shout down any attempts at fraud. They knew that they were playing an unequal match. With the referee being in total support of one team, the opposition was ready to seize the ball at any moment for play to discontinue. Jampassdie encouraged the spread of this rumour.

Election evening came with an uneasy calm. The radio announced that campaigns were going to fold up with the president's speech. It was clear that the President had homework to do in order to counteract the damage done by the poisonous declarations of Mr Jampassdie. He had been forced into competition and he had to be convincing to win back public opinion. With the multiparty set up, the old method of declaring a victory for the Head of State without convincing the electorate was now obsolete. After the usual news jingle, the awaited speech went thus:

"Kutumians, Kutumians, fellow country-men. We have reached the peak of our democratic process and tomorrow is the day for us all to consolidate this achievement. This message is addressed to all Kutumians without regard to partisan feelings because we are one, an indivisible people.

From independence until recently, we enjoyed peace and growth as we lived as one people with one sense of direction. But when pressure was brought to bear on us to introduce a multiparty system, I gave everyone a chance. Tomorrow is the day for us to separate truth from lies, to sieve the chaff from the mixture.

You will see that this change was just for the sake of change because the ruling party remains very strong and is even enjoying more popularity now than before the introduction of pluralism. All our comrades know that these power thirsty young men formed parties as an easy means to seizing power. To most of them, power is synonymous with food. Tomorrow, every right-thinking Kutumian must use the ballot box to ensure that this country not pass unto the hands of inexperienced adventurers. Today such persons claim to talk with divine piety. Don't be deceived by such empty declarations. On the pulpit, they talk piety clothed in immaculate glamorous white gowns, but underneath their minds are throbbing with different intentions. Because these adventurers have never had opportunities to be tested, they can deceive you with all sorts of angelic promises. Give them the chance and we will all regret the damage to our achievements. They will take us back to where we started. The abbreviation of the opposition party is indicative of their intention to ruin this country if they get to power. The NLP stands for 'No Love for the People.' So do not take them seriously.

We are expected to move forward on our political path rather than regress. Yesterday, we were accused of autocracy. When we brought in democracy, some mischievous citizens took advantage of this to install anarchy. I will not tolerate any anarchy in this country. It is often said that if you serve food to a pig on a clean tray, it will prefer to throw it down and eat it from the bare ground. I have served us clean democracy but some people eating it are contaminated. Don't give them a chance tomorrow.

Our development is a gradual process. We cannot have automatic change on a single day. We are progressing in our development according to the means available to us. We started with the struggle for independence; now we have gone to democracy. Give me your confidence again so that we can now galvanise all our energies towards development. We could not have achieved all three at a go!

To the youths, I promise to see to it that more jobs are created. I shall personally supervise this. The civil service should know that I have a plan for decentralisation that will benefit each and all so that increments are swift. I shall also see to it that your working conditions are made better. Salary scales shall be revisited. I have not been preaching ethics for the sake of preaching. All authorities who embezzle state funds shall be judged and sent to prison and their properties seized and auctioned. The women, as mothers of the nation, should know that my next five-year development plan shall give them pride of first place. I will create many women's centres and equip them with functional facilities. These centres will train women in many economic domains, empowering them and giving them a chance to share in moulding the *political life of the country. Those in public offices shall enjoy appointments and shall be given more priority to run for elected posts.*

These are promises from the father and founder of the nation, your incumbent, who has the might and means to put all of these into practice. You all know me as a man of action. Renew your confidence in me and Kutuma shall be a new paradise on earth."

Even if democracy had not yielded any fruits in this land, such a speech as this, unheard of in the history of Kutuma, meant that things really were changing. It was surprising that the roaring voice of the leopard could become so soft and musical to the sheep. Was this patriotism or merely election talk? When someone is starving and a benefactor comes and promises him a heavy delicious meal, all he can do is to swallow his spit and sit to wait and see. This is how Kutumians received the Head of State's speech.

That night, even though all rigging dispositions had been put in place, the President still thought of taking further occult measures. He went to the shrine of one of his power patrons and was told to visit the cemetery at midnight where the Prince of Power would communicate with him from the world of the dead and bless him for the event. He was reminded that he would have to take off all his clothes before he stepped onto the cemetery ground. He was asked to meet all the requirements which, because this was a strategic moment, would be very heavy. The most important one was that he should leave a heavy parcel on the grave and rise without looking behind as soon as he heard the voice of the Prince of Power.

He went out set for this mystical mission, taking along with him no companion. As soon as he got near the graveyard, he stripped himself naked in readiness to receive the prince. Then he knelt down and repeated the invocation, while pouring the libation of wine on the grave:

"Prince of Power, your servant is soliciting your intervention. Hear my supplication and come forward. The moment is crucial as I have challenges tomorrow. Make it possible that only my voice should be heard and that everyone, even my opponent, should follow my directives. As I talk, my head is touching the ground because you are lightening and fire. Come forth with mercy on my plea and not with damnation. My words are few," Utum Tar implored.

A barely audible voice replied, "Your desire has been heard and accorded. Place your earthly gift on my grave and look up for I have so permitted you!"

As he looked towards the direction of the voice, he saw a tall masked figure all dressed in white, with a large head wrapped in unkempt hair. The figure spoke while occasionally drinking some liquid from a calabash and blowing out fire vapour. What an awful sight this was!

"Now place your gift and turn and leave immediately. Your wish has been fulfilled. You dare not look behind," the voice concluded.

When he returned home, he had a few hours of sleep. The frightful image of the ghost kept flashing through his mind in nightmares as he slept. At times he dreamt that he was being pushed down into a grave by that frightful image.

This immediate apparition of the Prince meant that his appointment as foreseen by his fortune teller had worked. The spirit world was not a matter of imagination. It was a concrete reality. He rose early for morning mass before going to vote. He was quite reassured that all the noise made by his opponents was just a passing wind. They were mere flies buzzing around the body of a stout horse. Did they think they could change the man who had brought change? This was not possible.

Chapter Fourteen

P rior to this day, the prevailing hysteria could have made one believe that this would be a special day, unlike any others. It could be imagined that on such a day, the sun might turn red or green or any other colour. Would it be like the apocalyptic biblical day of total confusion when the dead and the living would both walk the streets? No, this was far from it. The morning of Election Day was quite a normal one. *Chopli* the bird played its normal time-keeping role, announcing the daybreak as did the cock. All domestic life went about busily in its routine manner. Shopkeepers opened their stores early to do some fast business before the injunction hour of 8a.m required them to shut their stalls. Fervent Christians went to church for Sunday worship. The slight difference was that bidding prayers centred on the need for peace in the country. The church service on this day was earlier than usual to permit people to come out early.

The difference was that campaigning was over and people were not crowding together like before. There was a sort of reverential silence and low peak in all conversations. People were heeding the instructions from the Head of Administration that no gathering should be found anywhere on this day, lest it be treated as a disturbance of the public peace. The army and police had been mobilised in all the corners of the republic to ensure that order prevailed.

Everything was in place for the election. Ballot boxes had been dispatched to all the polling stations well ahead of time. In enclave areas, militants had been paid to carry them on their heads and trek the long distances. Wherever these boxes went, security officers accompanied them. The opposition also took nothing for granted. They sent their representative to ascertain that all was well in their favour

At the Ndindi polling station, where Jampassdie had to cast his vote, the ballot box was displayed in the open yard of the market square. The Great Ruling Party did this to show the world that this country was a model in transparency. All the parties were represented in the various commissions.

Despite the injunction order against gatherings, some of Jampassdie's thugs decided to loiter around the main entrance into the polling stations. Their aim was to pinch the illiterate voters and remind them of the colour of their ballot papers. Some of the militants, despite every good faith, had difficulty learning their lessons. Though this colour had been explained to them over and over during campaign rallies, there was still much ignorance of the procedure. This was the case with Nini Fukun. The thug did the rehearsal exercise with her several times, but when she had to do a little test she kept failing.

"You will be given three cards, one is red, one is white, and one is green. Choose only the green one which is as fresh as a cocoyam leaf. You will find a bag hanging down on the wall to your right. This is a waste paper bag meant for dirty things. This is where you will throw away the other two dirty and useless ballot papers which both belong to the party in power. They belong to the selfish politicians who have caused us a lot of suffering and frustration. Take only that nice green one, that of the party of hope, that of Comrade Jampassdie, and put it gently into the envelope in your hand. Then move outside calmly and proudly to drop it into the ballot box, in plain sight of everybody. If you do just what I have told you, Mama, then you will shoot down the dictator because that green ballot paper has more power than a gun. Have you understood me, Mama?"

"Yes, my son," she answered.

"If yes, can you repeat all that I have explained to you, so that I can be sure that you will follow the instructions correctly?" the thug asked.

"I think you have said that I should put some papers that I will be given into an envelope. Then I will put all of them into a dirty bag and walk out as proudly as one who has caught an elephant. Is this not in short the long story you have been singing into my ears?" Mama replied with confidence.

"No, Mama. If you drop all the papers into one envelope and leave them in the waste bag, you have not voted. This will be wasteful participation. Remember to put only the green one into the envelope. However, if you get there and find that you are a bit confused, ask our party representative, Kum, to go into the booth and help you. Do not accept assistance from any other person. Ask only for Kum."

When Ni Fukun got to the polling station, she started quite well. She was given the three ballot papers. She got into the secret booth but then became very confused. When she saw the waste bag, she reached her hand inside and took out more ballot papers. She then came out with both hands full. Evidently there was a mixture of all colours, but those of the ruling party seemed to predominate. On seeing this, Kum of the NLP jumped up smartly and rushed towards her shouting:

"Mother! No! Get back into the booth and I will guide you."

Without wasting any time, he was already in the secret booth with the woman where he took out the ballot paper of his party and put it into the envelope. Then they both came out. This is when it occurred to Befi, the representative of the ruling party, that some foul play must have taken place. She raised the alarm, arguing that an interested party was not supposed to go into the booth to make a choice for a voter .In truth Befi had lost vigilance because a nap had caught her eyelids and she had dozed off. The previous evening she had consumed a lot of the free campaign drinks provided by the minister and had slept late in the service of one of the campaign team members from the capital. With the call to this other militant duty, she was not allowed to continue to sleep by her bed mate. She had struggled hard to put sleep off, but since nature cannot be cheated, sleep had overpowered her. Even as she tried to keep her eyes open, she was half-asleep. When she was overtaken, she bent her head down for a nap. This was when the incident occurred. It was only then that she raised the alarm against foul play.

An argument ensued, setting the stage for fighting. Voices were raised and spectators started gathering. When word of the tense situation got to the police station, troops of armed officers came in ready to disperse any rioters. Knowing that this was not a good day for risk-taking, some people escaped as soon as they caught sight of the police truck. Order returned to the polling station, and the voting exercise went on without further disturbance. This incident was a trick of the opposition, trying to pull a fast one on the ruling party; everyone in the political game has to device his own winning strategy.

But the ruling party, the organiser of the tournament, could not easily be outmatched. In Fenajul's palace, it was a one party show. The ballot box was kept in the *Fon's* conference room and his royal highness himself sat there supervising the undertakings. He was bent on having nothing short of a 100% score for the ruling party. All guards, notables, queens, princes and princesses in royal regalia came out and cast their votes. The ballot box was placed at the entrance to the sacred shrine of *Nesalajiki*, a goddess who punished any sort of betrayal. So any vote against the party supported by the *Fon* was believed to be a sort of betrayal that could invite the wrath of the goddess. Even with this cultural check, the *Fon* had to be sure that there were no adventurers who damned the consequences of the wrath of the *Nesalajiki* goddess. That is why he insisted that the ballot box be placed where he could personally supervise the casting of votes. Here you were not given three ballot papers, so there was no room for error. To make the process easy, only the papers of the ruling party were given out. At the end of the day, all the other ballot papers were bundled and stuffed into the waste bag. This arrangement was possible because no one could ever oppose the decision of the *Fon*. What's more, the palace was removed from the main settlement and it took a great deal of trekking to get there on rough, rocky paths. The opposition had to be very careful not to transport its intoxication for change into a conservative environment. Therefore, the voting exercise at the palace was more a formality than the challenging exercise it was in the other polling stations. The exercise lasted less than an hour, so the rest of the day was spent idling and waiting for the official closing hour for other polling stations across the Republic.

At 6 pm, crowds of people started forming around the major polling stations for the vote counting exercise. To prepare well for this important phase, kerosene lamps had been provided. They were the only sure source of light in the Ndindi locality. Individuals had armed their torches with new bulbs and batteries to be sure that transparency prevailed. Against security instructions, the crowds surrounded the restraining officers, each one with ears pricked for the reading of results.

When all was set, the person doing the reading dipped his hand into the box, took out one ballot paper and read it out to the hearing of all. As he pronounced the names of the contesting parties there was a sort of rhythmic beat:

NLP, NLP, NLP, KUP

NLP, NLP, NLP, KUP

KUP, NLP, NLP, NLP

Given the total focus on this exercise, thieves could have come into the village and made away with valuables unnoticed. Some local thieves actually did profit from the circumstances to break into some houses. The excitement was such that even children sneaked out of their homes to join their parents at the polling stations. Even little Ngong, the baby-sitter, had abandoned the baby alone in the house to be part of the evening show though he could not for certain explain what was happening. Wearing a rubber gun on his neck, he had chosen a very conspicuous position where he sat on the floor, nodding to the NLP and KUP song with no worry as to the outcome.

Much to the embarrassment of the ruling party, the opposition took the lead at the Ndindi polling station with a landslide margin. After the counting exercise, all the statistics were summed up and filled into results sheets signed by the supervisory authorities and representatives of the various parties. There were firm instructions to the public by the Head of Administration that these tentative results should not be taken as final because they were still to be confirmed by the final vote counting commission. The public should not be surprised if the final result was altered slightly from what they had just heard. This announcement created feelings of misgivings amongst critical minds within the opposition. They worried that the results were to pass through the laboratory of the state for screening.

From every polling station, all roads led to the Head of Administration's office. The crowds drifted from the polling station to this new centre of gravity and kept vigil. Ballot papers from distant polling stations took the whole night to get to the Head of Administration. Whenever a delegation was noticed arriving, the public huddled together with anxiety to learn the results. Anxious voices directed their question to their own representatives.

"How do things look?" the question went.

"NLP is topping very largely," the answer came.

Such answers sent members of the opposition wild with jubilation. The answer changed when the delegation from the palace arrived.

"How was it there?"

"Who can fight a lion in its den? The ruling party did it with no challenger to dare!" This answer animated diehards of the ruling party who had remained quiet for so long.

Controversy erupted in a distant polling station. The representative of the opposition came with one copy of the results sheet, while the official representative of the delegation, a member of the ruling party, had a totally different one. This tuned into a real embarrassment for the opposition representative who could not understand what had transpired. He had spent the whole day with the rest of the members and had no memory of signing this form that convincingly bore his signature. The official submission was the opposite of the final results that he had in his hand. The ruling party now appeared to be winning a landslide victory. When and how had it happened? Could something have transpired when he went to ease himself shortly after the counting exercise? Had the original results been switched during the wining and dining party hosted by the district chairman of the ruling party? All these questions crossed his mind with no clear answers. He felt bad when members of his party ridiculed him, saying that he had been offered something to oil his lips and keep quiet about well organised fraud.

"This was not the right person to send to represent us. Any bit of money could buy his conscience over," someone remarked.

"He has eaten *okro* soup and if things go the opposite way against our party he will pay for it with his head," comments went on.

The innocent representative retired to his home with unexplained guilt and presented his case to God, the Judge of the faultless.

Within opposition circles, the diehard militants did not see things that way. They immediately cried foul and ordered the population to rally in protest against the fraud. In less than no time, the arena of the Head of Administration was transformed into a rallying ground. Speaker after speaker denounced the act. They threatened to take the Head of Administration hostage if the right results were not released. He would not be allowed to move from his house to the National Headquarters. Other voices even suggested that the whole office should be burnt down. Some young men started voluntary contributions to raise money for petrol. Political tension these days was like fuel ready to be transformed into an unquenchable conflagration.

The Head of Administration mustered his courage and came out to address the angry youths and reassure them that there was nothing to worry about. He diplomatically explained to them that the opposition was winning and that any act of violence would be detrimental to this victory, possibly leading to the total cancelation of the result. Yet all that comforting talk was like throwing water on a duck's back. The mob insisted that it needed to see the original retain sheets and nothing short of that. Tension kept mounting. A young man appeared from nowhere with a gallon of fuel and a match, preparing for the demonstration lesson to take place.

Just at that moment agitations were suddenly interrupted by the intervention of armed forces. The crowd was encircled from all directions by the police and tear gas was randomly exploded to send everyone away. At the same time, one of the officers opened fire, shooting wildly into the air. As the crowd was dispersed, some ten meters away there was mournful wailing. There had been no orders to shoot and kill and there was no intention to do so. Why then were there mournful voices?

In the direction of this cry, someone was lying down dead. A stray bullet had flown one hundred meters away and struck the innocent, peace-loving, and generous Mundama who had nothing to do with the political agitation. He was a neutral person going about his morning routine of wine tapping. He had set out from his house with his two calabashes on his shoulders hanging down on a bamboo. Little did he know that he was treading on death's path. Bebin Mundama had never had partisan feelings and had lived his life without regard to the political hysteria around him. If he usually went out and voted, it was simply to avoid later harassment from the police when his voters' card was checked on market days. To him, anyone could lead a country provided life remained quiet. Whether it was Utum Tar or Jampassdie who ruled Kutuma, what mattered to him was peace.

Despite his indifference, fate had today positioned him in the centre of Kutuma politics. His accidental death sent the public wild with weeping. People wept so much for him because he was a very generous man. He tapped very good palm wine, not for sale but just to entertain passers-by. He also was a gifted farmer who had very healthy yields. When he harvested his crops in times of scarcity, he helped most of the villagers with food. Little children called him *"tonton"* because he offered them ripe bananas, oranges and sugar cane from his farm. But this fateful morning he had become the victim of the electoral process of Kutuma. This was the seventh death since the advent of political pluralism, giving an average of one corpse per day out of God's seven days of creation.

The whole village lamented the loss of a good man. This left neither members of the ruling party nor the opposition indifferent. But the opposition stole the show, taking over the responsibility to organise his funeral. After all, he had died from a bullet that was intended for one of them. He was posthumously a comrade on the front for change.

The Head of Administration sent a condolence message on behalf of the Head of State to the bereaved family and provided some money for burial arrangements. Yet the opposition decided that this sacrificial lamb for democracy should only be interred after the results. There was no mortuary in Ndini village, but the indigenes had a method for preserving a corpse using fresh bulbs of the banana stem. In this style, Mundama's corpse was preserved pending the election results.

Chapter Fifteen

S ome people live all their life span on earth unnoticed, but when death comes they enjoy renowned honour posthumously. This was the case with Bebin Mundama. His death was a big event, especially as it had a political undertone. Members of the ruling party showed sympathy in order to cover up murder, while the opposition took advantage of his death to whip up sentiments of revolt. Prolonged "wake keeping" went on, animated by cultural dances of various types. People brought basins of *fufu,* vegetables and meat without being organized to do it. Who would deny that sympathy pulls together even diametrically opposed people? Was it just sympathy, or was there a strong force in the departed spirit of Bebin Mundama that pulled in crowds of mourners? The concern over his death could trigger all sorts of questions.

While all attention was now focused on this sad event, the Head of Administration smartly rounded up his election report and forwarded it to the national vote counting commission. The final version did not reflect the real situation as obtained in the polling stations. Every retain sheet was redone in favour of the ruling party. The submitted report was a total reversal of the original version. This was a calculated strategy so that in the event of any unnecessary protest from the opposition, it would be explained that there had been a typographical error where the names of the parties were wrongly positioned on the corresponding statistical tables. Where the ruling party had 25% and the opposition had 75%, the final result gave the ruling party 75%, the opposition 25%. A mistake could not be taken for fraud.

One week later, election excitement started dying down. People resumed their routine activities. But anxiety lingered on in individual minds. Jampassdie had collected all the results from polling stations all over the country and summed them up. The result was fascinatingly in his favour. He was leading with an estimated 80% of the vote compared with 20% for the ruling party. His secretariat hastily summed up everything and produced a tentative result that was published on tracts and pasted all over the country.

The Head of State learned of this unofficial result and was very bitter about it. The police boss sent out his boys to tear down any such tracts and burn them. The radio repeatedly warned that anybody caught in the act of pasting fake results would be arrested and severely dealt with, for this was a very undemocratic procedure in a nation which was out to set new standards for democracy.

Despite the warning, Jampassdie organised a rally to educate the masses on the right conduct to adopt before, during and after the proclamation of results. Foreseeing the usual fraudulent drama that had so far maintained the Head of State in power, he prepared his militants well ahead of time for reprisal.

Political town criers sounded their whistles and horns as it was usual when summoning the public for a rally. In less than no time there was an intimidating population. Before the orators could start any messages of manipulation of the public the police was already there with tear gas and gunshots.

There were no deaths this time, but many people were arrested. Jampassdie was placed under house arrest while most of his thugs and advisers were locked up in police cells. No one was allowed to go into or come out of Jampassdie's compound. The house was searched and any instruments of communication such as the radio and telephone were confiscated. Whenever his family was running out of provision, the military brought in supplies. The intention was not to starve him to death. Rather, he was considered a necessary evil in the attempt to feign democracy, so he had to be encouraged to live on. But in order not to disturb the reign of the 'King', he was to live on in a cage. Those in police cells didn't have it easy. The conditions were quite appalling. The inmates slept on cold cement floors in over-crowded rooms meant for chronic criminals. Oxygen was a delicacy, for there was only one tiny hole serving as a window. The toilet was just a little bucket to be used by everyone and it sometimes got full to the brim and overflew, spilling faeces to the floor. One inmate was assigned every morning to dispose of the content of the bucket. Stubborn ones were asked to scoop the over spilt matter from the ground with their bare hands and return it to the buckets. Occasionally, they were all brought out for interrogation and asked to sign undertakings of respect to state orders.

Female inmates were better treated, for they were allowed to take a bath at least once every two days. The only pathetic case was that of Ngong's breastfeeding mother, who could only breastfeed her daughter when permitted. When Ngong brought the baby, he sat sorrowfully on the bench outside waiting for the mother to emerge from the cell. A little mischievous, he would pinch the baby on its buttocks so that it would shout and hasten the police to open the cell. The mother on the other hand suffered great pains at night when her breasts were full and needed to be drained. One of her comrades tried to help by sucking out the milk and spitting it to the ground. But this temporal relief could not replace the natural sucking. When the baby came and was breastfed, it would do itself and its mother good, for she felt much at ease for some time. On some nights, the baby would cry, keeping its father and Ngong sitting up all night. This poor soul was again an innocent victim of the democracy process. The police remained insensitive to the plight of inmates. The relationship deteriorated when the ladies insulted a police attendant after he pushed the nursing mother with brutality as she was delaying outside with the baby.

"Idiot, an old man of your age with a wife and children is pushing a nursing mother without shame! How is this woman different from yours? You should be ashamed of yourself!" a shouting voice came out of the cell.

"For now, you feel comfortable because you are putting on a khaki shirt and trousers and holding a gun. Do you think you can remain for ever in that nasty job? When retirement comes you shall find yourself worse than those of us who are not working like you. You have to respect us, for we are your mothers. You are already behaving like one suffering from a curse." Angry voices shouted out variations of these phrases.

A good policeman was trained to bear these accusations silently. Even if it was his mother, wife, daughter or girlfriend, he was supposed to remain unmoved. That was a policeman's lot, to take commands without hesitation.

The traditional mortuary could not continue to house the remains of Bebin Mundama. The already decaying body needed to be buried even without the much awaited results. Nothing was filtering out from the National Vote Counting Commission.

Despite the prevailing tension, friends, family members and sympathisers of the Bebin decided to give him a befitting burial by cultural standards. The Honourable Minister decided to make it a big event by sending a live cow to be slaughtered for refreshment. This was a political gesture of appeasement, but the interest in feasting was not as warm as during elections because this was not an event for merry-making.

Early that morning, stout youths came to his compound with grave-digging implements. Family members provided the cooked corn mixed with groundnuts traditionally eaten during a burial. When the youths started digging, they noticed a strange phenomenon. After the first attempt to till, barely a few centimetres deep, there was a rock that prevented further the digging. They decided to change spots. They started digging again and met another rocky obstacle. They tried about ten times but were always blocked. In one case, not only did they meet terrible stony obstacles, but a viper jumped out and chased people before disappearing into the bush.

This strange situation was reported to the palace, and the *Fon* decided to invite his soothsayers to investigate the situation. They concluded that Mundama's spirit was angry and needed appeasement before it would accept burial. Further, failing to bury the body could lead to even greater calamity for the whole country. The great *Ghetasingangha* looked for appeasement herbs and the family members provided some fowls and salt for a special burial ritual. The *Fon's* emissary, a dangerous juju known as *buli*, set out for that compound. When the masquerade got there, wild with ecstasy, children, women and the uninitiated fled into hiding. The juju executed some smart displays with spears and cutlasses in both hands and landed on the spot to be dug. It buried the royal spear in the ground and then pulled it back out. This was a signal that it was now safe to dig. Then the leader of the *Besingangha* came forward with the calabash in his hand and said the following incantation:

"Beben Mundama, we want your spirit to rest. It is one week now since you did not cross the bridge and meet your ancestors. May the one who caused your hasty departure from this world find no peace! Here are the goats and fowls for your appeasement. As you look back on us, protect those of us who were dear to you and smash the skulls of those who did you wrong. You see and know our hearts better than we see ourselves. May you find a better life amongst your ancestors!" Then he poured some palm wine into the hole created by the spear.

Digging started and, to the utter surprise of everyone, there were no more obstacles. Once they finished digging, it was time to lower the remains. This is usually a moment of intense emotions. Women started shouting as if the Bebin had just died. The lone sister jumped and feigned entering into the grave, but was held back by strong, hefty young men. As she had missed the grave, she could not miss rolling on the ground. Freeing herself from the grip of the young men, she fell to the ground and began rolling from one end of the compound to the other. After letting her venting her emotions, two women went and helped her up, wiping her tears gently. Once the grave was filled to the brim, there was a light drizzle which was interpreted as a shower of blessings. Next, they fired guns in honour of the Bebin's departure. The sound of gun shots invited the gendarmes, who rushed in and went about seizing the guns from their owners. Anyone caught with a gun was charged with preparing a bloody overthrow of the government. As if the killing of Bebin Mundama was not enough, many more unfortunate victims were taken to the police cells.

Chapter Sixteen

The proclamation of the much-awaited results was long overdue. A pregnancy that goes beyond its normal term becomes a cause for concern. The surgeon would need to induce contractions. But who could do this for the Kutuma democratic process when every opposition force was being held in check? When Jampassdie was living encircled by arms? Maybe the people counted only on the invisible hand of fate.

Despite the falsification of the original reports, the Head of State understood that his hypnotic political strength was waning. His field collaborators had done everything within their powers to maintain the status quo. But he knew that his position was shaky. Once again, he decided to seek occult advice. He decided to try another great witch doctor because the graveyard rituals had not yielded the desired results. His confidential adviser advised him to move far away to Mbuk, a remote village where a renowned old man lived. The President agreed, confirming that those around town had all become charlatans in a quest for wealth. They had lost their natural powers owing to the love for money. After the poor results for his party, he had a good reason to doubt the efficiency of the graveyard scene on the eve of elections. He questioned whether the Great One from the beyond, whom he had seen vomiting fire vapour, was even from the spirit world. When failure meets a believer of fragile faith, he starts doubting his god. The President for once questioned his god.

For the Head of State to move to such a remote locality there was need for some preparation. Knowing that at a certain point they would have to trek for many kilometres, he sent for good rubber boots and a raincoat. He also needed a disguise because he would meet many people who would wonder what was taking such a personality to the end of the world. To this end, he bought a pair of sunglasses and a dark cap that covered his head right down to his ears.

When all was set, he left in the company of three confidential guards and his advisers. They were all seriously disguised to ensure that no acquaintance could recognize them. The first lap was on a track much like the road to Ndindi. So as not to arouse curiosity, they did not take a luxurious car. They hired a ramshackle Land Rover that befitted such roads. After riding all night long, they reached the end of the navigable road. From there, they used the oldest means of transport, where salvation comes from one's two legs. After four hours of trekking, all the members of the delegation were drenched in sweat. At first, the Head of State enjoyed it, claiming it was an opportunity for a slim course. But when he found his feet all getting sore, he understood that the struggle to remain in power was quite costly. At a certain point, his legs could scarcely carry him on, but, with encouragement from his companions, he kept on trying. When they got to the Mbuk Bridge, the President nearly gave up. It was a rough rope and bamboo crossing, measuring about twenty metres, which swung its pedestrians menacingly as the wind swung it from left to right. When the Head of State saw this obstacle, he was gripped with fright and felt the urge to ease himself. He contemplated turning back. But after encouragement from the companions, he attempted the crossing. Being someone very allergic to heights, he felt as if the bridge was turning him upside down as it swayed with every step taken. In the middle of the bridge, he had palpitations and quivered with fright. "Do not look down into the river. Hold your head up," his companions urged him. Finally the test was over, and he found himself on the other side of the bridge, breathing very fast from fear.

The company then sat down to have lunch and replenish the lost energy. Just at this moment, an old man came out from the nearby forest with palm wine. The sweet scent and frothing foam were so enticing that the Head of State felt he needed to quench his thirst immediately with this sap from the natural sieve of the palm. In his early, modest years, he used to enjoy this special drink and now it was a change from the imported wine that he drank throughout his stay in high office. It was very natural to drink from the tapper's calabash and horn cups. At the end, the Head of State stretched out a big bank note as payment and Pa shuddered with fright, complaining that he had no change. But surprisingly, the Head of State told him that this was all for him because this drink was of more value than the money. Was this a humane gesture or campaign strategy?

When this entertainment was over, the tapper moved away into the village, torn between surprise and joy at the luck he had had that afternoon. The first person he met and talked it over with was the ward president of Jampassdie's party. The latter gave this information some critical thought and was keen to know who these august guests were. When at last they arrived and he observed that this was the Head of State and his entourage, he alerted a few people, amongst them the very *Wutangang* that the President was coming to meet.

The Head of State was warmly received at the *Wutangang's* compound where they killed a large cock and provided them with a good meal and proper lodgings. As *Wutangang* was a great man with many wives and children, the whole compound bustling with activity in the reception of the august guests. One of the wives, Iyafi, decided to prepare a fast trap by making sure that it was her daughter who served the guests their food, prepared warm water for bathing and met their other needs. This was enough enticement for the Head of State who did not hate such an opportunity. The girl directed him to his living quarters where he was to spend the night. Before going to bed, the *Wutangang* granted him an audience and learned about his worry. He cautioned that, for a proper diagnosis of the problem, it was better that they slept and got up early in the morning. The practice of soothsaying was generally carried out in the morning. Behaving as if he did not know the great personality, he formally asked for all his names, claiming that this would permit him to start working spiritually that night. In this way, he would get the necessary directives for handling the problem.

Deep into the night, while the Head of State was busy in his room, serious secret political transactions went on outside. The president of the opposition met the *Wutangang* and pleaded with him that this was the time to make history in Kutuma. He echoed the opposition's position against the ruling party, asking the *Wutangang* to do all in his powers to put an end to dictatorship.

"You know I cannot kill. My profession is to save people's lives, not kill," he said with an apologetic voice.

"We are not asking you to eliminate him. We are saying that, if there is medicine to do the opposite of keeping him in power, give him that. Give him medicine to make him relinquish his grip on the throne. That is the wisest thing to do. If we brutally eliminate him here through poisoning, the whole village might be sent to prison or wiped out," the ward president concluded.

With every partisan feeling in him, the *Wutangang* did not need much persuasion. He even proposed a safe way to proceed to his comrades. Every strategy was to be contained in the fortune-telling of the next day. He carefully planned ahead of time how to work on the Head of State's mind the next day. People like the *Wutangang* still existed in the country, people whose ideological stand is stronger than individual sentiment and interest. Although he could do the expedient thing and have all the wealth he could ever acquire in a lifetime, he acted in the interest of his party and not his personal wellbeing.

Early in the morning, the President and his body guards were summoned into the *Wutangang's* shrine. It was a little grove behind his house, characterised by some special medicinal stones for sacrifices, carvings, a little stream flowing out of a spring, and noises from assorted aquatic animals. The *Wutangang* wore bangles on his arms and his face was painted with chalk and charcoal. In his left hand, he held a bag which, when pressed, issued a hissing sound like the noise of a chick. In his right hand, he held a bell. When he rang the bell three times, he pressed the bag and listened. Then he went ahead to interpret the message from the spirit world.

"Kiring, kiring, kiring!" went the bell.

"Mighty One from the great beyond, here is your servant, Utum Tar, who wants you to further anoint his throne with cam wood so that he can stay on in power. If it is pleasing to your high office that he remains in power, guide me on what to tell him." (*He pressed the bag and listened to the hiss.*)

He said, "I should tell you that the moment is not favourable for you. You have enjoyed this advantage for a long while and your period of fortune is nearly over. There is a black cloud covering your luck and you have turned fate to your disadvantage."

"Please, *Wutangang*, find out from the Great One of the spirit world what that wrong could be and how it could be mended," Utum Tar pleaded.

"He wants to know what exactly he has done wrong and whether his mistakes can be forgiven. A human being can make mistakes for he is not a spirit. But we can wash them away. What wrong did he do? How can we cleanse him from his iniquity?" The *Wutangang* placed his request and the usual hissing sound followed.

"I should tell you that you have killed people whose spirits are now working against you in their world. Your own powerful spirit got lodged in the body of one of these people. When he was killed, your power spirit flew off with his. This is how you lost your strength to remain in power. It further says that cleansing you is no easy matter. No material sacrifices can atone for the death of that dreadful spirit which vanished with your power. You may have to make very expensive personal sacrifices to regain what has been lost," the *Wutangang* said.

"Please, Papa, get the precise details of what I should do. I am ready for any sacrifice. I am ready to give up all my wealth to remain in power. If you can do anything for me, I am ready to pay any price that is demanded." Utum Tar appeared quite agitated now.

"You can see that he is crying like a baby for help. He is desperate and needs clemency from the spirits. Tell him, Great One; those possibilities open to him to make amends." Following the hissing sound, the Wutangang proceeded to interpret the message from the underworld to the eager audience.

"You are lucky but you need to make strong decisions. You have been given a range of options. The first one is that you would have to lose your manhood. This means that you would have to idle away the rest of your life as a eunuch. If you accept this option, then you will have all the power you need but would have nothing to do with the world of ladies! The next one is that you would have to make love in public with a mad woman. For this to be effective, you will have to wait for the time when there is a large crowd, like in a market place, to do so. You would not do this once, but repeatedly for seven days. The next option is that you go about mad and naked for seven years. During this period, you would sleep in abandoned houses and on rubbish heaps. When this time is over, you would regain your mental health and get back your power. The last and least costly one is that you surrender your post of President to any of your rivals. After one term in office, your electorate will judge that your reign was better and return you to power. By then, they would have seen that your opponent was not as holy as he claimed he was. Decide the best of these options."

These predictions from the *Wutangang* sent shock waves down the spine of President Utum Tar, rendering him dumbfounded. For close to fifteen minutes, he behaved as if he had already been caught by the third option. He stamped his feet on the ground, clapped his hands, stretched his head and looked around in utter surprise. Faced with agitation of this degree, his companions requested that they retire to his room for some reflection in order to arrive at a proper decision.

They comforted the President, permitting him to return to good reasoning. Then they decided to go through the various options.

The first one was just unthinkable for a man who had strong relish for women. Did this mean that his previous night had been his last taste of a woman? And what a great night it had been with a young woman No, God forbid! As for the second and third, choosing the one was as ugly as choosing the other. It is just like a man being asked to choose which form of death he prefers: hanging or by being burnt alive. Both tortures before death were equally awful. Then this last option, which looked good, was total privation and humiliation to the Founder of the Republic. He had never imagined such an idea. How could he surrender to his boastful inferior who had spent all his time castigating his reign? After careful insight into this option, he came to the conclusion that this could be the best. It all depended on how he introduced his resignation to his fellow countrymen. What sounded like a cowardly decision could be converted to a heroic one. His technical adviser promised that, when they returned, he was going to work out a good procedure for this, so that when the breaking news was released, many militants of the opposition party would send him motions of support. To make it sweeter, it would be arranged in such a way that he remained the leader of the party and the party would be given a greater status as it was the first ever party that was created in the history of Kutuma. With this renewed confidence, they returned to the *wutangang* to pronounce the president's choice.

"Have you made up your mind at last?" the *wutangang* enquired.

"Yes, we have," the President replied.

"Which of the options have you decided on?"

"The last," Utum Tar reluctantly answered.

"Good," the Wutangang cut in. "Whatever wishes you solicit here will be directed to the spirits. This stone is the dwelling place of all our ancestry. You will place your hand on the stone while pronouncing your wish. This immediately becomes a pact that you are signing with the spirits. That is the most essential part. Thereafter, I will proceed with other rituals now and after you are gone. Go ahead, place your hand on the stone and pronounce your wish, repeating after me." At this the Wutangang asked Utum Tar to repeat after him:

"I, Utum Tar, do solemnly pronounce here before the ancestors that I will relinquish hold of my throne to my opponent. May they be witnesses of my sacrifice and do me the favour of bringing me back to power when my rival fails."

Every ritual has a price. Utum Tar even had to pay for relinquishing his power. He was charged to provide the essentials for sacrifice. Not having brought any live sacrificial items, he had to replace every need with money. At the end, he was given a concoction to drink and warned to abide by the oath, lest he invite the wrath of the gods on him and the entire republic.

Not very happy with the outcome of this journey, they travelled back home in very low spirits hardly talking to one another. Deeply drowned in thought, the Head of State crossed the hanging bridge in a dream mood and only remembered afterward that he had done so. When life starts getting sour, all accompanying circumstances seem unfavourable. Even the weather was not sympathetic. That night there was a torrential down pour accompanied by a disastrous thunder storm. They struggled on, having no place for shelter. By the time they got to where the car had been parked, they were all in a sorry mood. As if the rain had been carefully timed, it ceased abruptly when they jumped out on the motorable road. They undid the wet dresses but, with his goggles and cap, he remained disguised. They rode back in a moody frame of mind until they got to the palace.

That night, Utum Tar called the chairman of the National Vote Counting Commission to know for formality sake what the general performance was. He was told that nothing had changed. Even the polling station in the Presidency had given an embarrassing result. In one of the polling stations, the ruling party had scored 0%, meaning that even its representatives had not cast votes in its favour. This was quite dangerous. The Head of State seemed surrounded by lions.

Chapter Seventeen

From weeks to months and from months to one full year, there were no official results. The electorate had given up any interest in the election. This was a trick to hang on to power a little longer. No information was filtering out of political circles about the Head of State's intentions.

The police and the military had reinforced security measures. Jampassdie remained under house arrest, and some of his activists were confined to prison cells. There was a generalised social malaise. Every professional group was anxious for a strike, but there was no room for trade unions to vent their feelings. Surprisingly, even the military was tired of going on aimless missions to quell an uprising that was neither seen nor felt anywhere. They were tired of sleeping in the open every night while in search of political suspects.

Kutumians were used to their lot. A wonderful people, they could pretend that all was well even when nothing was. Every day, although they were disgruntled, people went about their daily tasks. Yet the atmosphere was one of social discontent. Children returned from school with empty exercise books, saying that the teachers spent time conversing in the corridors or sleeping on the tables. There were no drugs in the hospitals and, if a nurse was not motivated, she would not attend to a patient. Prices of most basic commodities shot up. Even farm produce became expensive, as the farmer needed to compensate for the higher cost of industrial products.

Then a strange plague known as *come no go* befell the whole country. This was an incurable skin disease that was resistant to all drugs. Scientists claimed that it was a fatal sexually transmitted disease. All its victims had rashes that lacerated the body, leaving scars. The opposition explained that this was a malediction brought on the country by bad governance. Church ministers thought it was a sign of the apocalypse because God was angry with man's sinfulness. One man, Prophet Joshua, took advantage of the situation, going door to door preaching repentance.

Prophet Joshua could not arrange a public crusade for fear of the police's reaction. "Repent, dear brothers and sisters, for the time of the Lord is at hand." Youth in search of employment, frustrated civil servants and childless couples joined his Ministry of Salvation, draining the mainstream churches of their Christians. Some of the converts were truly convinced that the world was ending. The prophet even attempted to prophesy the day of the week, but mentioned neither the month nor the year. He claimed that the world would end on a Friday, so each Friday his worshippers were ready; however, the date proved as unpredictable as the Presidential election results.

Certain unusual events gave credence to his prophesies. Firstly, after a very difficult delivery, a young woman gave birth to Siamese twins with two heads and four legs. The mother survived through God's mercy, for she gave birth in the hospital waiting room, unattended by any nurse. She had come to the hospital with severe labour pains, but the striking nurses ignored her. It was only after the delivery of her strange baby that they rushed to her, more out of embarrassment than sympathy, and picked up the infant which, fortunately, was a still birth. To the prophet, this was an ill omen, warning those whose faith was not strong.

Next, a woman stole a bag of groundnuts from another's farm and started bleating like a goat. She had been caught by a powerful medicine that was planted in that farm against thieves. When this trouble befell her, she had already sold the bag of groundnuts and held only a few grains in her hand as explanation for her guilt. Other medicine men attempted to reverse the medicine but could not. She became dumb and went about bleating with the groundnuts in her fist.

Her plight was similar to that of a policeman who received a bribe of five hundred francs from a driver. This policeman was so notorious for harassing drivers that one man prepared to take vengeance on him. He came along with a bank note carefully arranged with a spell. When he handed the note to the policeman, it immediately transformed into a chick that could never part with him. It got stuck to his palm, and every effort to remove it failed. These were the many signs of the time in the Founding Father's beloved country.

Every wonder was possible in this Republic. Finally, two women were caught making love. How on earth could a woman be making love with another woman if this was not the end of the world? It was difficult for the ordinary man to make sense of this. How could a woman play the role of a man successfully? This pair was taken to the palace to confess their act, but surprisingly, they declared that they were deeply in love. Following threats on their lives, they apologised for breaking the norm and said that they would stop. These ladies were beautiful enough to make perfect wives for young men, but they were misusing their female roles. This reminded many people that Young Boy really was well-informed when he occasionally cracked jokes about this phenomenon.

Political scientists saw these oddities as a transition to a Third Republic, the prophet interpreted them as the apocalypse, and traditionalists saw them as a curse needing cleansing. Which of these interpretations was right?

Chapter Eighteen

When a boil matures to the bursting point, nothing can stop it from exploding. It can burst to bring relief or kill the patient. The boil of Kutuma was ready to explode.

One evening after the citizens had retired to their homesteads, feeling hopeless, a strange news jingle sounded over the radio. Unlike the one that ushered in democracy, this one was a mixture of the news jingle and various songs in praise of the Head of State. It was easy to guess that they were preparing to announce the victory of the ruling party. The tunes went on and on with occasional breaks, but no comment was forth coming. Then the journalist on duty made the introduction, "The Head of State addresses the Nation."

"Kutumians, Kutumians, fellow countrymen, I have decided to step down from my office of Head of State in order to foster the democracy, which I willingly offered to my country. I have decided to hand over power to the opposition as proof of my democratic attitude. I had this intention ten years ago, but I needed enough time to prepare my succession. I am convinced that my successor is sufficiently groomed to carry out this mission successfully. To ensure that this transition goes smoothly, I am calling on the Supreme Council to organise the swearing in ceremony within twenty four hours. In the meantime the police and the army should ensure that there is peace all over the country. I will leave the Presidency this very evening and occupy my private family lodge in Shisha quarters. I promise that, as a lover of this land, I will remain available as a political adviser to my successor in order to ensure that our country continues to grow. My comrades in the great ruling party should know that, even though I have stepped down from power, we are still together. I have resigned from power, not from the party. One cannot rule for as long as I have done without unintentionally displeasing some people. To those who were not very satisfied with my reign, I appeal for forgiveness. To my supporters and close collaborators, I remain highly indebted."

This bizarre news turned night into day. Everyone was out on the street, especially members of the opposition. To be sure this was a reality, members of the opposition rushed to Jampassdie's house to witness his release from house arrest. It was real. The police on guard had walked away. There was singing and beating of all sorts of objects in celebration of the collapse of tyranny. Oddly enough, contrary to previous practice, everyone was in jubilation, even members of the ruling party, the police, and the army.

This jubilation was barely momentary because just one problem had been solved; that of the ousting of the dictator. But he had thrown the democratic bone to a host of hungry dogs believing that he had chosen one brave dog to eat it all, the undesignated successor. The new question that came up was, who was this successor? He had tactfully designated no one to take over from him. Who then was the Supreme Court going to swear in?

Chapter Nineteen

News of the resignation solicited reactions from all strata of society.

The army, without its honorary head, went loose. The first sign was at Jampassdie's house where those on duty immediately withdrew. This permitted militants and sympathisers to flow in quickly and celebrate the good news with Jampassdie. His compound was jammed with people that night, flocking in from every direction. While some hugged and congratulated him, his rivals did so as mere flash show and lip service because the real combat was just to begin.

The next day at the NLP headquarters, all the militants assembled to take a stand as to the vacant post. The Head of State had left an open competition with no rules of the game.

When deliberations opened, the master of ceremony read the agenda containing a lone item; that of the proposal for the candidate to fill the highest post of the state. This is when real hidden intentions emerged. In less than five minutes, there were more than twenty self-nominations. "I nominate myself" was repeated over twenty times.

Once again, this meeting turned into a forum for quarrels and animosities. While some reasonable voices thought that Jampassdie, who had sacrificed a lot, should be rewarded by his followers, others said that the post of party chairman was enough for him. Many speakers were vocal on the matter.

"We should not get this God-given opportunity and squander it by enthroning another dictator. From the time multiparty set up started, we have had only Mr Jampassdie at the head of the NL.P. Does it mean we lack leaders? Let us not give this impression to the world. Being a party leader does not guarantee becoming the head of state. Let us set the good example of democracy by choosing from among the nominees one person to fill this vacancy."

"This is real contradiction of our position. Does it mean that we made an error to select him as a candidate at the last unpublished elections? Now that he even won and the results were not proclaimed, do we mean that if the out-going president had permitted the publication of the results would we have refused him from taking over the magistracy of the state?"

After listening to all this talk, the highly disappointed Jampassdie commented:

"If there is one thing that I can understand now, your choice of me as presidential candidate was because you thought I could never win, that dictatorship was going to continue as before. Now we are beginning to see our hypocrisy exposed to the open."

As voices rose to the sky, the meeting came to an end without any resolution.

The military for its part started its own share of confusion. Later on in the evening of the next day, there were sporadic gun shots from a nearby neighbourhood. Soon, information went round that a young military officer had proclaimed himself Head of a military junta. This had been done without consulting his superior officers. Most of his badge mates had joined in and saluted this initiative. This was an individual who had been keeping the seal of an ammunition warehouse. Before day break, there were said to be over three different military factions, each claiming supremacy in state affairs.

The most appalling leadership that came up on the third day was an unorganised, nation-wide civil disobedience led by teenagers who undertook to burn up most major buildings and set up road blocks. This was a generation crisis. The youth had written down their grievances against their elders. These were carried on placards and written on walls of buildings, and anywhere that the eye could catch. Some of the grievances read as follows:

1. We are a sacrificed generation.
2. Our elders have not set us good examples of sacrifice for the nation.
3. Down with a greedy set of old persons.
4. Mother Kutuma has been milked to the dying point. What shall its calves suck?
5. Kutuma is bubbling hot *fufu* for the bravest eater to seize with his bare hands.
6. Kutuma is hot *fufu* that can peel off your gums and fingers.

This rioting pulled up a huge following. Shops were broken into. There was indescribable looting of property. Now that there was no public security to bother about life and property, everything went upside down. This youth force grew to such prominence that it overpowered the military factions that had attempted to take over power. At first, only their intimidating numbers caused other power aspirants to give up. Soon they were able to seize guns from the military.

The situation could be likened to the mythical Zombie that was at the genesis of Kutuma. It is said that people of Kutuma were first settled somewhere out of this land. Then, because there were so many deaths where they were, they decided to move to a new land. Its elders fasted for seven nights and seven days. Then God sent a spirit man to lead them to their promised land. This man had no head, but had all his body parts and, therefore, moved to just any direction. The people suffered behind the zombie until it finally reached the present site and pronounced that this was their final point. Then it melted into thin air, just as it had appeared. That is how the ancestors settled here. It was still believed that, one day, the spirit man would re-appear for another migration to take place.

Now, the Zombie had resurfaced many centuries later in a different form. It was no longer a mobile, headless figure, but was a state with no head, with its citizens just wandering with no directive of leadership. Was there need for another headless Zombie to come and cause Kutuma people to move out of this country in modern times? If this were possible, which other land in modern times remained virgin where a set of migrants like these ones could settle? Their destiny lay in their hands, and their heads were all on their shoulders to build a better nation, rather than reducing it to ashes.

The fuel for the burning of the state was readily available. All the filling stations that had been seized became the property of the rioters and fuel was carried along in cans for the easy burning of tyres on the high way. Road blocks were set up at many points. Some government buildings were set on fire.

Most of the citizens remained indoors and soon started running out of provision. Delicate health care resulted in deaths and all the dead were buried on the spot.

The only public places that were allowed to function were church houses because the rioting youth said that people were allowed to go to church and repent for their sins.

The death toll resulting from misery after three months was more than could be registered in an open confrontation. Worse of all, everyone was soon becoming everyone else's enemy. The gangsters that had fled from prison after the state of lawlessness became a threat to everyone. Most rich homes were invaded; the rich peoples' daughters and wives were raped. The *cam-no-go* virus tripled within a very short time.

Soon everyone needed order to return, but no one was welcome as a leader.

With an atmosphere of total insecurity people went to bed very early. Attitudes were adjusted to suit the changing times. The usual drinking houses only functioned discreetly. Beer was sold privately and the price of a bottle doubled. With total suspicion prevailing everywhere, a neighbour needed to announce and identify him or herself before a door could be opened.

One evening, after a heavy down pour of rain, a rainbow appeared. This natural sign in the Kutuma belief system presaged an important happening. Generally this was a sign of peace that could also announce the arrival of a great personality like a king. People attempted to interpret this sign but with no accuracy.

Then one day, a young man had an inspiration to salvage his country. This was Yumfuyenfu, 'God's bird', the boy whose mother was shot at the launching of the N.L.P. At twenty five, he had grown to maturity and had had a university education through a philanthropist. His father, Mr Yeye, committed suicide shortly after the murder of his wife. All along the little boy had lived with Fundoh, the leper, who had miraculously got well, cured by a certain prophet. Yumfuyenfu, the age mate of Kutuma democracy had come of age to perform a divine role to his country.

Yumfu undertook a crusade to consult the opinion of prominent leaders and to seek ways to bring back order in the state. First, he met the youth leader who initiated the nation-wide riot and talked with him from a young man's perspective. All the youth bought into his idea that, after all this demonstration, there was need for a National Conference in which the youth would have to defend their interest. He appointed a committee to write out the youth's point of view in a memo entitled, "A Generation in Perdition." The consultation was long and penetrating. Many people heeded to the call of this chosen one. People who had lost their jobs through lay off took great advantage to vent out their venom.

Chapter Twenty

This new day was ushered in by bright weather. *Chopli* and all his companions of mirth announced this at dawn. The sun shone as if to brighten the charcoal and pieces of the broken Republic. And it penetrated into the minds of those that could mend the pieces.

The public came out en masse, heeding to the call for talks from the chosen one, Yumfu. All footsteps were once again in the direction of the Catholic School field. But today the actors, participants and agenda were not the same. The key players were the youths of Nyumfu's age bracket and neutral people in the former game. In the past, this arena had served as a starting point in the lead speaker's political destiny when he survived the massacre of the launch. He and his peers who were born in the period of that memorable event, only knew about this place from the stories recounted to them by their parents and elders. And like any children born in the crises of a political epidemic, they had been inoculated with the vaccine of change. This, therefore, gave them the impetus to work as hard as they had done.

When all was set, Nyumfu climbed on the elevation on which the flag post was affixed. Then in a very clear and authoritative voice he started delivering his message:

"Uwooh Uwooh Uwooh!" he saluted.

"Uwooh Uwooh Uwooh!" the audience responded in unison.

This was the traditional salute of intimacy amongst young people.

Then he went ahead, "I thank all of you who feel that this dear fatherland has to be saved from total destruction. I am no orator, no authority, but I am commanded from within to propose to my brothers the need to return to good humour and save our fatherland. When a man falls on a slippery road, he is always very careful not to fall on that same road a second time.

The wounds of our democratic process should not be seen as ulcers that cannot heal. We are our own doctors. Let us give tolerance a chance. In this new consideration, no one is more a Kutumian than another one. Let us sit down at one table and right our wrongs. This time, we should avoid all the errors of the past, for we have learnt from our mistakes. In this new consideration, we must bear in mind that not everyone must be a leader.

To rebuild the house, we have to get back to its foundation, by reviewing our constitution. I am thus inviting our eminent scholars of this domain to work on this document with the seriousness that it deserves before we go any further. The next step is that we need a steering committee to prepare for the new republic that we are setting up here. Let us be careful not to call it a conventional government so as not to provoke some wounds. The essence of this is that our state cannot remain headless like our mythical *wutalumgba*. This steering committee will handle the affairs of the country until real free and fair democratic elections are conducted. From the shame of the world, let us move up to a level of pride that can serve as a model to other nations. Our target should be to pass from the level of a developing nation to an emerging economy of prominence. Everyone has a chance to make it. We have the potential to change our position in the world ranking. Yesterday we were the beauty of the world, the princess that every colonial power needed to woo. They married us, but with time there was divorce through independence. Prior to this, we had blamed all our failures on the white man. Independence came and put us to the test of self-rule. This permitted us to know ourselves, to understand our own limitations. We can see for ourselves that since independence, we have been responsible for our slow growth. No white man has ruled here since independence. We have our destinies in our hands, and it is left to us to take advantage of our fall and walk straight forever."

This talk was received with prolonged applause. It was evident that, after the period of broken pieces, everyone was yearning for peace. Proof of this was the fact that after his talk, no dissenting voices came up with contrary views. On the contrary speaker after speaker came up and only corroborated his proposal.

As if commanded by a magical wand, a steering committee made up of highly neutral personalities of observable integrity was nominated. Nyumfu surprisingly turned down his own nomination to head the committee. Instead, he promised to occupy the modest post of adviser. It seemed the god of Kutuma had returned to guide the people once again on this new migration that remained on one spot and only re-conquered itself.

The steering committee, led by Reverend Pastor Mbanga, was to begin work the very next day. It was given a road map which had as priority actions to foster reconciliation amongst the various interest groups of Kutuma, to work out an acceptable constitution for the republic, and to prepare a level ground for free and fair elections. And so did a new Kutuma begin.

People come and go, yet the country remains. The rocky hills, the fertile lowlands, the deep rivers, *Chopli* and early risers were still there like before. But the Founding Father was bed ridden with AIDS and political frustration. He had been reduced to a large skull on a pack of bones. Jampassdie was sweating from high blood pressure, born of betrayal. But he still looked physically fit and hoped to strike a deal with the new political class. The queen of all parties, the welcome of all guests, Natti had joined a Pentecostal movement that was moving from door-to-door preaching repentance and abstinence. She wore a headscarf which covered her forehead and came to the edges of her eyebrows. Her conversion came on the day she had her HIV status declared as positive. Youngboy continued to share his jokes with the youths. His therapeutic formula was very necessary in the rebuilding of broken minds.

Glossary of Local Words

1 *manyi*, a mother of twins
2 *Fon*, a traditional ruler
3 *fufu*, food prepared from corn flour
4 *mbeh*, an address of honour to the *fon*
5 *Mungang*, traditional medicine from herbs
6 *Wutangang*, a derivative of *mungang referring severally to a soothsayer, doctor, magician, etc.*
7 *ghetasingangha*, the plural of *wutangang*
8 *Bebin*, an address of respect to an adult who owns a compound
9 *bayam-sellam*, retail traders
10 *nzolo*, football slang where a dribbler sends the ball between the legs of his opponent.
11 *Kwifon*, the highest regulatory institution in the area of jurisdiction of a fon
12 *Famla*, a sect whose members acquire wealth and power through the death of relatives
13 *nkang*, liquor brewed from fermented corn
14 *gwofukang*, the dried skin of a bush baby. 'gwo' means 'skin' and 'fukang' means
 'bush baby'
15 *chopli*, the clock bird
16 *mama*, an address of honour to an elderly woman, meaning 'mother'
17 *papa*, the masculine of *mama*
18 *nesalajiki*, a traditional goddess, with one long breast reaching the ground, who brings punishment to rule breakers.